George Colman

The Clandestine Marriage

A Comedy in Five Acts

George Colman

The Clandestine Marriage
A Comedy in Five Acts

ISBN/EAN: 9783744787222

Printed in Europe, USA, Canada, Australia, Japan

Cover: Foto ©Andreas Hilbeck / pixelio.de

More available books at **www.hansebooks.com**

No. XXXVIII.

FRENCH'S STANDARD DRAMA

———•———

THE

CLANDESTINE MARRIAGE.

A Comedy

IN FIVE ACTS.

BY GEORGE COLMAN, THE ELDER.

WITH THE STAGE BUSINESS, CAST OF CHARACTERS, COS-
TUMES, RELATIVE POSITIONS, &c.

———◆———

NEW YORK:

SAMUEL FRENCH, PUBLISHER;

122 Nassau Street, (Up Stairs.)

CAST OF CHARACTERS.

	Covent Garden, 1824.	Pork May, 1843
Lord Ogleby	Mr. W. Farren.	Mr. Placide.
Sir John Melvil	" Baker.	" Abbott.
Sterling	" Fawcett.	" Bellamy.
Lovewell	" Cooper.	" Lovell.
Canton	" Yates.	" Fisher.
Brush	" Jones.	" E. Shaw
Sergeant Flower	" Claremont.	
Traverse		
Trueman	" Mears.	
John (a Servant)	" Heath.	" King.
Mrs. Heidelberg	Mrs. Davenport.	Mrs. Vernen.
Miss Sterling	" Faucit.	Mrs. Hunt.
Fanny	Miss Jones.	Miss Buloid.
Betty		Mrs. Knight.
Chambermaid		Mrs. Lovell.
Trusty		Miss Bedford.

** *In order to abridge the time of the representation of this piece, the parts of Sergeant Flower and his legal companions are now usually omitted.*

COSTUMES.

LORD OGLEBY.—*First dress:*—Flowered satin dressing-gown, a bow of white satin riband on his head. *Second dress:*—Full court dress, with spangles. &c.

SIR JOHN MELVIL.—Dress hat, blue dress coat, white waistcoat, white breeches. white silk stockings, and shoes.

STERLING.—Cocked hat, brown coat, waistcoat, and breeches; white stockings, and shoes.

LOVEWELL.—Round black hat, blue coat, white waistcoat, black breeches, black silk stockings, and shoes.

CANTON.—*First dress:*—Cocked hat, light coat trimmed with black, a belt, huge French postillion's boots, his hair in papers. *Second dress:*—White coat, light drab breeches, very short at the knees, light and spotted silk stockings and shoes.

BRUSH.—Olive green coat, buff waistcoat, flesh coloured breeches, and silk stockings, and shoes.

MRS. HEIDELBERG.—*First dress:*—Dark flowered gown, a flat and very wide gipsy hat. *Second dress:*—Flowered silk gown (very large pattern) trimmed with scarlet, ruffles, high cap, and long fliers. *Third dress:*—Common robe-de-chambre, &c.

MISS STERLING.—White satin.

FANNY.—White muslin, trimmed with white satin.

BETTY.—Flowered cotton gown, black silk apron.

EXITS AND ENTRANCES.

R. means *Right;* L. *Left:* R. D. *Right Door;* L. D. *Left Door* S. E *Second Entrance;* U. E. *Upper Entrance;* M. D. *Middle Door*

RELATIVE POSITIONS.

R., means *Right;* L., *Left;* C., *Centre;* R. C., *Right of Centre,* L. C., *Left of Centre.*

N.B. Passages marked with Inverted Commas, *are usually omitted in the representation.*

EDITORIAL INTRODUCTION.

As a finished specimen of dramatic art, the comedy of " The Clandestine Marriage" holds a very high rank. Mr. Peake, the biographer of the Colmans, says it may be put, in the list of the acting drama, next in merit to the " School for Scandal"; and though we are somewhat doubtful as to the justice of this classification, we cannot pronounce the estimate an extravagant one.

The title-page of the original edition of the comedy bears the names of George Colman and David Garrick as the authors; but there can be little doubt that by far the greater part of it was written by the former. Garrick, though possessing some of the most essential qualities of the successful playwright, had not much true literary ability; while Colman was not only an accomplished writer, but a good classical scholar. The whole outline of the plot of this piece appears to have been his, as well as the idea of the principal characters. In a letter to Garrick inclosing a rough draft of the general scheme of the play, together with loose hints of acts and scenes, Colman, after giving a pretty clear foreshadowing of the story as it now stands, concludes by remarking: " Of the *dénouement* I have not as yet even conceived those imperfect ideas I have got of some other parts. Think of the whole: and think in my train, if it appears worth while; and when you have thrown your thoughts on paper as I have mine, we will lay our heads together, Brother Bayes."

Upon the subject of Garrick's dramatic partnership, George Colman the Younger communicates the following facts: " In respect to the report of Garrick having written the entire character of *Lord Ogleby*, my father once told me it was not true; that, as an instance to the contrary, he (my father) wrote the whole of Ogleby's first scene. He also informed me that one of

Garrick's greatest merits in this work (and it is a great one), was planning the incidents in the last act; the alarm of the families through the means of Mrs. Heidelberg and Miss Sterling, and bringing forward the various characters from their beds to pro duce an explanation, and the catastrophe. I regret that when my father imparted this, I did not make further inquiry; but I was then 'a moonish youth', and troubled my head little or nothing about the matter. He always talked, however, of the play, as a joint production. Dramatic connoisseurs may discover the styles of authors; and there are few such connoisseurs who will not, I think, be of my opinion, that far the greater part of the dialogue in this comedy came from my father's pen, rather than that of Garrick."

The part of *Lord Ogleby* having been intended for Garrick, his refusal to play it seems to have produced a temporary interruption of friendly feeling between him and Colman. But real infirmities had incapacitated the great actor from representing fictitious ones; and dreading to encounter the fatigues of suc cessive performances, he resigned the part to King, who acquired deserved celebrity in it, and vindicated the propriety of his se · lection. But the most distinguished representative of this character is Mr. Farren, whose personation, according to the unanimous testimony of his critics, is one of the most perfect pictures that the stage has ever offered. The character itself is drawn with consummate skill, and carefully perfected. It is unequal led in its excellence among the list of superannuated beaus and ancient rakes, which the drama can show. " Judgment, originality, and fidelity, are combined in the delineation ; and though the old lord's follies and foibles be in themselves sufficiently despicable, yet by investing him with generous and humane principles, he is preserved from our contempt."

" This comedy," says Richard Cumberland, "is one of the most pleasing and legitimate in our language. It does not sparkle with brilliant, but misplaced wit ; it does not convulse us by the distortions of buffoonery, nor startle us by extravagance of incident or character ; but the genuine taste that can pardon the absence of these modern beauties, will find abundant compensation in its nature, ease, and temperate vivacity. As long as these qualities maintain their attraction, The Clandestine Marriage will support its high reputation."

The "Clandestine Marriage" was originally produced at Drury Lane Theatre early in 1766, and had a remarkably successful run. Farren's *Lord Ogleby* is still one of the most attractive personations of the London stage. In view of the eminent merits of this comedy as an acting piece, it is a little surprising that it is not oftener performed in this country. Is the absence of a great *Lord Ogleby* the cause? Yet both Placide and Burton are fully competent to the part. The late Mr. Finn would have played it to perfection. He was the best antiquated beau we have ever seen.

The comic characters of the play are drawn with much neatness and skill. *Canton* is the most amusing of parasites; and the passages between him and his venerable coxcomb of a master, are buoyant with humour and vivacity, and tell well in the representation. *Mrs. Heidelberg* is the prototype of Sheridan's Mrs. Malaprop; but she is a character little known and appreciated out of English society. The impudent valet, *Brush*, seems to have suggested the not dissimilar character of *Trip*, in the "School for Scandal." His aping of his master's foibles and vices tends to expose their genuine absurdity, and contributes to the truthful effect of the whole dramatic grouping. The character of *Sterling* is sketched with great spirit, and is not without its parallels even in our own day and country.

In conclusion we may remark, that there are few comedies that will better bear a searching critical analysis of their dramatic merits than the "Clandestine Marriage." Perhaps the one great defect of the plot is the absence of a clearly adequate motive for the concealment of the marriage; and *Sir John Melvil* very justly intimates at the close, that a little candour on the part of the married pair would have saved a world of perplexity and uneasiness. But then that very perplexity was essential to the dramatist's purposes. The error lay in not making its necessity greater and more obvious.

CLANDESTINE MARRIAGE.

ACT I.

SCENE 1.—*A Room in Sterling's House.—Miss Fanny and Betty meeting.*

Enter BETTY.

Betty. Ma'am! Miss Fanny! Ma'am!

Fanny. What's the matter, Betty?

Betty. (c) Oh, la! ma'am! as sure as I'm alive, here is your husband—

Fanny. Hush! my dear Betty; if anybody in the house should hear you, I am ruined.

Betty. Mercy on me! it has frightened me to such a degree, that my heart is come up to my mouth.—But as I was a-saying, ma'am, here's that dear, sweet—

Fanny. Have a care, Betty.

Betty. Lord! I am bewitched, I think—But as I was a-saying, ma'am, here's Mr. Lovewell just come from London.

Fanny. Indeed!

Betty. Yes, indeed, and indeed, ma'am, he is! I saw him crossing the court-yard in his boots.

Fanny. I am glad to hear it.—But pray, now, my dear Betty, be cautious. Don't mention that word again, on any account. You know we have agreed never to drop any expressions of that sort, for fear of an accident.

Betty. Dear ma'am, you may depend upon me. There is not a more trustier creature on the face of the earth, than I am. Though I say it, I am as secret as the grave—and if it's never told till I tell it, it may remain untold till doom's-day for Betty.

Fanny. I know you are faithful—but in our circum
stances, we cannot be too careful.

Betty. Very true, ma'am! and yet I vow and protest
there's more plague than pleasure with a secret; espe
cially if a body mayn't mention it to four or five of one's
particular acquaintance.

Fanny. Do but keep this secret a little while longer
and then, I hope, you may mention it to anybody.—Mr
Lovewell will acquaint the family with the nature of our
situation as soon as possible.

Betty. The sooner the better, I believe; for if he does
not tell it, there's a little tell-tale I know of, will come and
tell it for him.

Fanny. Fie, Betty!   [*Blushing.*

Betty. Ah! you may well blush.—But you're not so
sick, and so pale, and so wan, and so many qualms—

Fanny. Have done! I shall be quite angry with you.

Betty. Angry!—Bless the dear puppet! I am sure I
shall love it as much as if it was my own.—I meant no
harm, heaven knows.

Fanny. Well, say no more of this—it makes me uneasy.
All I have to ask of you is, to be faithful and secret, and
not to reveal this matter, till we disclose it to the family
ourselves.

Betty. Me reveal it! If I say a word, I wish I may be
burned. I would not do you any harm for the world—
And as for Mr. Lovewell, I am sure I have loved the dear
gentleman ever since he got a tide-waiter's place for my
brother—But let me tell you both, you must leave off your
soft looks to each other, and your whispers, and your
glances, and your always sitting next to one another at
dinner, and your long walks together in the evenings. For
my part, if I had not been in the secret, I should have
known you were a pair of lovers, at least, if not man and
wife, as—

Fanny. See there, now! again. Pray be careful.

Betty. Well—well, nobody hears me. Man and wife
—I'll say no more—what I tell you is very true, for all
that.

Lovewell. [*Calling without,* L.] William!

Betty. Hark! I hear your husband—

Fanny What!

Betty. I say, here comes Mr. Lovewell—Mind the cau-
.ion I give you—I'll be whipped, now, if you are not the
first person he sees or speaks to in the family. However,
if you choose it, it's nothing at all to me—as you sow, you
must reap—as you brew, so you must bake. I'll e'en slip
down the back stairs, and leave you together. [*Exit*, R.

Fanny. I see, I see I shall never have a moment's ease
till our marriage is made public. New distresses crowd
in upon me every day. The solicitude of my mind sinks
my spirits, preys upon my health, and destroys every comfort of my life. It shall be revealed, let what will be the
consequence

Enter LOVEWELL. L.

Lov. My love! How's this? In tears?—Indeed, this
is too much. You promised me to support your spirits,
and to wait the determination of our fortune with patience. For my sake, for your own, be comforted!—
Why will you study to add to our uneasiness and perplexity?

Fanny. Oh, Mr. Lovewell; the indelicacy of a secret
marriage grows every day more and more shocking to
me. I walk about the house like a guilty wretch: I ima
gine myself the object of the suspicion of the whole family; and am under the perpetual terrors of a shameful
detection.

Lov. Indeed, indeed, you are to blame. The amiable
delicacy of your temper, and your quick sensibility, only
serve to make you unhappy. To clear up this affair properly to Mr. Sterling, is the continual employment of my
thoughts. Everything now is in a fair train. It begins
to grow ripe for a discovery; and I have no doubt of its
concluding to the satisfaction of ourselves, of your father,
and the whole family.

Fanny. End how it will, I am resolved it shall end soon
—very soon—I would not live another week in this agony
of mind, to be mistress of the universe.

Lov. Do not be too violent, neither. Do not let us disturb the joy of your sister's marriage with the tumult this
matter may occasion!—I have brought letters from Lord
Ogleby and Sir John Melvil to Mr. Sterling.—They will
be here this evening—and I dare say, within this hour.

Fanny. I am sorry for it.

Lov. Why so?

Fanny. No matter—Only let us disclose our marriage immediately!

Lov. As soon as possible.

Fanny. But directly.

Lov. In a few days, you may depend upon it.

Fanny. To-night—or to-morrow morning.

Lov. That, I fear, will be impracticable.

Fanny. Nay, but you must.

Lov. Must! Why?

Fanny. Indeed you must. I have the most alarming reasons for it.

Lov. Alarming indeed! for they alarm me, even before I am acquainted with them. What are they?

Fanny. I cannot tell you.

Lov. Not tell me?

Fanny. Not at present. When all is settled, you shall be acquainted with everything.

Lov. Sorry they are coming!—Must be discovered!— What can all this mean?—Is it possible you can have any reasons that need be concealed from me?

Fanny. Do not disturb yourself with conjectures—but rest assured, that though you are unable to divine the cause, the consequence of a discovery, be what it will, cannot be attended with half the miseries of the present interval.

Lov. You put me upon the rack. I would do anything to make you easy—But you know your father's temper. Money (you will excuse my frankness) is the spring of all his actions, which nothing but the idea of acquiring nobility or magnificence can ever make him forego—and these he thinks his money will purchase.—You know too your aunt's (Mrs. Heidelberg's) notions of the splendour of high life, her contempt for everything that does not relish of what she calls quality; and that from the vast fortune in her hands, by her late husband, she absolutely governs Mr. Sterling and the whole family: now, if they come to the knowledge of this affair too abruptly, they might, perhaps, be incensed beyond all hopes of reconciliation.

Fanny But if they are made acquainted with it otherwise than by ourselves, it will be ten times worse : and a discovery grows every day more probable. The whole family have long suspected our affection. We are also in the power of a foolish maid-servant ; and if we may even depend on her fidelity, we cannot answer for her discretion. Discover it, therefore, immediately, lest some accident should bring it to light, and involve us in additional disgrace.

Lov. Well, well—I mean to discover it soon, but would not do it precipitately. I have more than once sounded Mr. Sterling about it, and will attempt him more seriously the next opportunity. But my principal hopes are these: My relationship to Lord Ogleby, and his having placed me with your father, have been, you know, the first link in the chain of this connexion between the two families ; in consequence of which, I am at present in high favour with all parties : while they all remain thus well-affected to me, I propose to lay our case before the old lord ; and if I can prevail on him to mediate in this affair, I make no doubt but he will be able to appease your father ; and, being a lord and a man of quality, I am sure he may bring Mrs. Heidelberg into good humour at any time. Let me beg you, therefore, to have but a little patience, as, you see, we are upon the very eve of a discovery, that must probably be to our advantage.

Fanny. Manage it your own way. I am persuaded.

Lov. But in the mean time make yourself easy.

Fanny. As easy as I can, I will. We had better not remain together any longer at present. Think of this business, and let me know how you proceed.

Lov. Depend on my care. But, pray, be cheerful.

Fanny. I will.   [*Going* R. *meets* STERLING *entering.*

Ster. (R.) Hey-day ! who have we got here ?

Fanny. [*Confused.*] Mr. Lovewell, sir.

Ster. And where are you going, hussey ?

Fanny. To my sister's chamber, sir.   [*Exit,* R.

Ster. (R. C.) Ah, Lovewell ! What ! always getting my foolish girl yonder in the corner ? Well, well—let us but once see her eldest sister fast married to Sir John Melvil, we'll soon provide a good husband for Fanny, I warrant you.

Lov. (C.) Would to heaven, sir, you would provide her one of my recommendation !

Ster. Yourself? eh, Lovewell!

Lov. With your pleasure, sir!

Ster. Mighty well!

Lov. And I flatter myself, that s. ch a proposal would not be very disagreeable to Miss Fanny.

Ster. Better and better!

Lov. And if I could but obtain your consent, sir—

Ster. What! you marry Fanny!—no, no—that will never do, Lovewell! You are a good boy, to be sure; I have a great value for you—but can't think of you for a son-in-law. There's no stuff in the case, no money, Lovewell.

Lov. My pretensions to fortune, indeed, are but moderate; but though not equal to splendour, sufficient to keep us above distress. Add to which, that I hope by diligence to increase it; and have love, honour—

Ster. But not the stuff, Lovewell! Add one little round 0 to the sum total of your fortune, and that will be the finest thing you can say to me. You know I've a regard for you—would do any thing to serve you—any thing on the footing of friendship—but—

Lov. If you think me worthy of your friendship, sir, be assured that there is no instance in which I should rate your friendship so highly.

Ster. Psha! psha! that's another thing, you know. Where money or interest is concerned, friendship is quite out of the question.

Lov. But where the happiness of a daughter is at stake, you would not scruple, sure, to sacrifice a little to her inclinations.

Ster. Inclinations! why, you would not persuade me that the girl is in love with you—eh, Lovewell?

Lov. I cannot absolutely answer for Miss Fanny, sir; but I am sure that the chief happiness or misery of my life depends entirely upon her.

Ster. Why, indeed now, if your kinsman, Lord Ogleby, would come down handsomely for you—but that's impossible—No, no—'twill never do—I must hear no more of this. Come, Lovewell, promise me that I shall hear no more of this.

Lov. [*Hesitating.*] I am afraid, sir, I should not be able to keep my word with you.

Ster. Why you would not offer to marry her without my consent! would you, Lovewell?

Lov. Marry her, sir!   [*Confused.*

Ster. Ay, marry her, sir! I know very well that a warm speech or two from such a dangerous young spark as you are, would go much farther towards persuading a silly girl to do what she has more than a month's mind to do, than twenty grave lectures from fathers and mothers, or uncles and aunts, to prevent her. But you would not, sure, be such a base fellow, such a treacherous young rogue, as to seduce my daughter's affections, and destroy the peace of my family in that manner. I must insist on it, that you give me your word not to marry her without my consent.

Lov. Sir—I—I—as to that—I—I—beg, sir—Pray, sir, excuse me on this subject at present.

Ster. Promise then, that you will carry this matter no further without my approbation.

Lov. You may depend on it, sir, that it shall go no further.

Ster. Well, well—that's enough—I'll take care of the rest, I warrant you. Come, come, let's have done with this nonsense. What's doing in town? Any news upon 'Change?

Lov. Nothing material.

Ster. And how are stocks?

Lov. Fell one and a half this morning.

Ster. Well, well—some good news from America, and they'll be up again. But how are Lord Ogleby and Sir John Melvil? When are we to expect them?

Lov. Very soon, sir. I came on purpose to give you their commands. Here are letters from both of them.
                              [*Giving letters.*

Ster. Let me see—let me see—'Slife, how his lordship's letter is perfumed!—It takes my breath away. [*Opening it.*] And French paper, too! with a fine border of flowers and flourishes—and a slippery gloss on it that dazzles one's eyes. " My dear Mr. Sterling." [*Reading.*] Mercy on me! His lordship writes a worse hand than a boy at his exercise. But how's this? Eh! " with you to-night!" —[*Reading.*]—" Lawyers to-morrow morning"—that's sudden, indeed.—Where's my sister Heidelberg? she

B

should know of this immediately. Here, John! Harry!
Thomas! [*Calling the Servants.*] Hark ye, Lovewell!
Lor. Sir!
Ster. Mind now, how I'll entertain his lordship and Sir
John—We'll show your fellows at the other end of the
town how we live in the city—They shall eat gold—and
drink gold—and lie in gold—here cook! butler! [*Calling.*]
What signifies your birth and education, and titles ? Money, money, that's the stuff that makes the great man in
this country.
Lov. Very true, sir!
Ster. True, sir! Why then have done with your nonsense of love and matrimony. You're not rich enough to
think of a wife yet. A man of business should mind nothing but his business.—Where are these fellows ? John!
Thomas! [*Calling.*] Get an estate, and a wife will follow
of course.—Ah! Lovewell! an English merchant is the
most respectable character in the universe. 'Slife, man,
a rich English merchant may make himself a match for the
daughter of a nabob. Where are all my rascals ? Here,
William!   [*Exit, calling,* R.
Lov. [c. *alone.*] So—as I suspected—quite averse to
the match, and likely to receive the news of it with great
displeasure. What's best to be done ? Let me see! Suppose I get Sir John Melvil to interest himself in this affair.
He may mention it to Lord Ogleby with a better grace
than I can, and more probably prevail on him to interfere
in it. Poor Fanny! It hurts me to see her so uneasy,
and her making a mystery of the cause adds to my anxiety. Something must be done on her account; for, at all
events, her solicitude shall be removed.   [*Exit,* R.

SCENE II.—*Another Apartment.*

MISS STERLING *and* MISS FANNY *sitting.*

Miss Ster. [*Both rise.*] Oh, my dear sister, say no more !
This is downright hypocrisy. You shall never convince
me that you don't envy me beyond measure. Well, after
all, it is extremely natural—it is impossible to be angry
with you.
Fanny. (R. C.) Indeed, sister, you have no cause.

Miss Ster. (l.. c. And you really pretend not to envy
me ?

Fanny. Not in the least.

Miss Ster. And you don't in the least wish that you were
just in my situation ?

Fanny. No, indeed, I don't. Why should I ?

Miss Ster. Why should you ? What ! on the brink of
marriage, fortune, title—But I had forgot—There's that
dear sweet creature Mr. Lovewell, in the case. You would
not break your faith with your true love now for the world,
I warrant you.

Fanny. Mr. Lovewell ! always Mr. Lovewell ! Lord,
what signifies Mr. Lovewell, sister ?

Miss Ster. Pretty peevish soul ! Oh, my dear, grave,
romantic sister ! a perfect philosopher in petticoats ! Love
and a cottage ! Eh, Fanny—Ah, give me indifference and
a coach and six !—

Fanny. And why not the coach and six without the indifference ? But, pray, when is this happy marriage of
yours to be celebrated ? I long to give you joy.

Miss Ster. In a day or two—I can't tell exactly—Oh,
my dear sister !—[*Aside.*] I must mortify her a little.—I
know you have a pretty taste. Pray give me your opinion
of my jewels. [*Goes back to the table and returns with jewels.*] How do you like the style of this *esclavage ?*

[*Shewing the jewels.*

Fanny. Extremely handsome, indeed, and well fancied.

Miss Ster. What d'ye think of these bracelets ? I shall
have a miniature of my father set round with diamonds,
to one, and Sir John's to the other. And this pair of ear-
rings ! set transparent ! here, the tops, you see, will take
off to wear in a morning, or in an undress—how do you
like them ?   [*Holding them up.*

Fanny. Very much, I assure you—Bless me, sister, you
have a prodigious quantity of jewels—you'll be the very
queen of diamonds.

Miss Ster. Ha! ha! ha! very well, my dear! I shall
be as fine as a little queen, indeed. I have a boquet to
come home to-morrow—made up of diamonds, and rubies,
and emeralds, and topazes, and amethysts—jewels of all
colours, green, red, blue, yellow, intermixed—the pret-
tiest thing you ever saw in your life! The jeweller says,

I shall set out with as many diamonds as anybody in town, except Lady Brilliant, and Polly—What d'ye call it, Lord Squander's kept mistress.

Fanny. But what are your wedding-clothes, sister?

Miss Ster. Oh, white and silver, to be sure, you know— I bought them at Sir Joseph Lutestring's, and sat above an hour in the parlour behind the shop, consulting Lady Lutestring about gold and silver stuffs, on purpose to mortify her.

Fanny. Fie, sister! how could you be so abominably provoking?

Miss Ster. Oh, I have no patience with the pride of your city-knight's ladies—Did you ever observe the airs of Lady Lutestring drest in the richest brocade out of her husband's shop, playing crown whist at Haberdasher's Hall —whilst the civil smirking Sir Joseph, with a snug wig trimmed round his broad face as close as a new-cut yew-hedge, and his shoes so black that they shine again, stands all day in his shop, fastened to his counter like a bad shilling?

Fanny. Indeed, indeed, sister, this is too much—If you talk at this rate, you will be absolutely a bye-word in the city—You must never venture on the inside of Temple-Bar again.

Miss Ster. Never do I desire it—never, my dear Fanny, I promise you. Oh, how I long to be transported to the dear regions of Grosvenor Square—far—far from the dull districts of Aldersgate, Cheap, Candlewick, and Farringdon Without and Within! My heart goes pit-a-pat at the very idea of being introduced at Court! gilt chariot! pie-balled horses!—laced liveries! and then the whispers buzzing round the circle—'Who is that young lady? who is she?' 'Lady Melvil, Ma'am!' Lady Melvil! My ears tingle at the sound. And then at Dinner, instead of my father perpetually asking—'Any news upon 'Change?'—to cry, 'Well, Sir John! anything new from Arthur's!'—or—to say to some other woman of quality, 'Was your ladyship at the Duchess of Rubber's last night? Did you call in at Lady Thunder's? In the immensity of the crowd I swear I did not see you—scarce a soul at the opera, last Saturday—shall I see you at St. James's next Thursday?' Oh, the dear Beau-Monde! I was born to move in the sphere of the great world.

Fanny. And so, in the midst of all this happiness, you have no compassion for me—no pity for us poor mortals in common life.

Miss Ster. [*Affectedly.*] You? You're above pity—you would not change conditions with me—You're over head and ears in love, you know. Nay, for that matter, if Mr. Lovewell and you come together, as I doubt not you will, you will live very comfortably, I dare say. He will mind his business—you'll employ yourself in the delightful care of your family—and once in a season, perhaps, you'll sit together in a front box at a benefit play, as we used to do at our dancing master's, you know—and perhaps I may meet you in the summer with some other citizens, at Tunbridge. For my part, I shall always entertain a proper regard for my relations. You sha'n't want my countenance, I assure you.

Fanny. Oh, you are too kind, sister!

Enter Mrs. Heidelberg, r.

Mrs. Hei. [*At entering.*] Here this evening!—I vow and pertest, we shall scarce have time to provide for them.—[*To Miss Ster.*] Oh, my dear! I am glad to see you're not quite in a dish-abille. Lord Ogleby and Sir John Melvil will be here to-night.   [*Fanny retires back and sits.*

Miss Ster. To-night, ma'am?

Mrs. Hei. Yes, my dear, to-night. Oh, put on a smarter cap, and change those ordinary ruffles!—Lord, I have such a deal to do, I shall scarce have time to slip on my Italian lutestring. Where is this dawdle of a housekeeper?

Enter Mrs. Trusty, l.

Oh, here, Trusty! do you know that people of quality are expected here this evening?

Trusty. Yes, ma'am.

Mrs. Hei. Well—Do you be sure, now, that every thing is done in the most genteelest manner—and to the honour of the family.

Trusty. Yes, ma'am.

Mrs. Hei. Well—but mind what I say to you.

Trusty. Yes, ma'am.

Mrs. Hei. His lordship is to lie in the chintz bed-chamber; d'ye hear? and Sir John in the blue damask room His lordship's valet-de-shamb in the opposite—

Trusty. But Mr. Lovewell is come down ; and you know that's his room, ma'am.

Mrs. Hei. Well, well ; Mr. Lovewell may make shift, or get a bed at the George. But hark ye, Trusty!

Trusty. Ma'am!

Mrs. Hei. Get the great dining-room in order as soon as possible. Unpaper the curtains, take the kivers off the couch and the chairs, and put the china figures on the mantle-piece immediately, and set their heads a-nodding.

Trusty. Yes, ma'am.

Mrs. Hei. Be gone, then! fly this instant. Where's my brother Sterling ?

Trusty. Talking to the butler, ma'am.

[Fanny rises and advances.

Mrs. Hei. (c.) Very well. [*Exit Trusty,* R.] Miss Fanny! I pertest I did not see you before. Lord, child, what's the matter with you ?

Fanny. (L.) With me! Nothing, ma'am!

Mrs. Hei. Bless me! Why, your face is as pale, and black, and yellow—of fifty colours, I pertest. And then you have dressed yourself as loose, and as big—I declare there is not such a thing to be seen, now, as a young woman with a fine waist—You all make yourselves as round as Mrs. Deputy Barter. Go, child!—You know the qualaty will be here by and bye—Go, and make yourself a little more fit to be seen. [*Exit Fanny,* L.] She is gone away in tears—absolutely crying, I vow and pertest. This ridiculous love! we must put a stop to it. It makes a perfect natural of the girl.

Miss Ster. (R. C.) Poor soul! she can't help it.

Mrs. Hei. Well, my dear; now I shall have an opportoonity of convincing you of the absurdity of what you was telling me concerning Sir John Melvil's behaviour to you.

Miss Ster. Oh, it gives me no manner of uneasiness. But, indeed, ma'am, I cannot be persuaded but that Sir John is an extremely cold lover. Such distant civility, grave looks, and lukewarm professions of esteem for me and the whole family! I have heard of flames and darts, but Sir John's is a passion of mere ice and snow.

Mrs. Hei. Oh, fie, my dear! I am perfectly ashamed of you. That's so like the notions of your poor sister. What

you complain of as coldness and indifference, is nothing
but the extreme gentilaty of his address, an exact pictur
of the manners of qualaty.

Miss Ster. Oh, he is the very mirror of complaisance !
full of formal bows and set speeches ! I declare, if there
was any violent passion on my side, I should be quite jealous of him.

Mrs. Hei. I say jealus, indeed ! Jealus of who, pray ?

Miss Ster. My sister Fanny. She seems a much greater
favourite than I am, and he pays her infinitely more attention, I assure you.

Mrs. Hie. Lord ! dy'ye think a man of fashion, as he
is, can't distinguish between the genteel and the wulgar
part of the famaly ?—Between you and your sister, for instance—or me and my brother ?—Be advised by me, child :
It is all purliteness and good breeding. Nobody know
the qualaty better than I do.

Miss Ster. In my mind, the old lord, his uncle, has ten
times more gallantry about him than Sir John. He is full
of attentions to the ladies, and smiles, and grins, and leers,
and ogles, and fills every wrinkle of his old wizen face
with comical expressions of tenderness. I think he would
make an admirable sweetheart.

Enter STERLING, L.

Ster. [*Entering.*] No fish ? Why, the pond was drag-
ged but yesterday morning. There's carp and trench in
the boat. Pox on't, if that dog Lovewell had any thought,
he would have brought down a turbot, or some of the
land-carriage mackerel.

Mrs. Hie. Lord, brother, I am afraid his lordship and Sir
John will not arrive while it is light.

Ster. I warrant you. But pray, sister Heidelberg, let
the turtle be dressed to-morrow, and some venison—and
let the gardener cut some pine-apples—and get out some
ice. I'll answer for wine, I warrant you. I'll give them
such a glass of Champagne as they never drank in their
lives--no, not at a duke's table.

Mrs. Hei. Pray, now, brother, mind how you behave. I
am always in a fright about you with people of qualaty
Take care that you don't fall asleep directly after supper,
as you commonly do. Take a good deal of snuff, and

that will keep you awake—and don't burst out with your
horrible loud horse-laughs. It is monstrous vulgar.

Ster. Never fear, sister! Who have we here !

Mrs. Hei. It is Mounseer Canton, the Swish gentleman,
that lives with his lordship, I vow and pertest.

Enter CANTON, L.

Ster. Ah, mounseer! your servant, I am very glad to
see you, mounseer.

Cant. (L.) Mosh oblige to Monsieur Sterling. Ma'am,
I am yours. Matemoiselle, I am yours. [*Bowing round.*

Mrs. Hei. (c.) Your humble servant, Mr. Cantoon!

Cant. (L.) I kiss your hands, matam.

Ster. Well, mounseer! and what news of your good
family ? When are we to see his Lordship and Sir John ?

Cant. Monsieur Sterling! Milor Ogleby and Sir Jean
Melvil will be here in one quarter-hour.

Ster. I am glad to hear it.

Mrs. Hei. Oh, I am perdigious glad to hear it. Being
so late, I was afeard of some accident. Will you please
to have anything, Mr. Cantoon, after your journey ?

Cant. No, I tank you, ma'am.

Mrs. Hei. Shall I go and show you the apartments, sir ?

Cant. You do me great honneur, ma'am.

Mrs. H. Come, then.—[*To Miss Ster.*] Come, my dear !

Canton crosses to R., and exits with Mrs. H. and Miss Ster.,
bowing and protesting they do him too much honneur.

Ster. Pox on't, it's almost dark. It will be too late to
go round the garden this evening. However, I will carry
them to take a peep at my fine canal at least, I am determined.   [*Exit,* R.

END OF ACT ONE.

——◆——

ACT II.

SCENE I.—*An Ante-chamber to Lord Ogleby's Bed-cham-*
ber. Table with chocolate, and small case for medicines.

Enter BRUSH, *my Lord's Valet-de-Chambre, and* STERLING'S
Chambermaid.

Brush. You shall stay, my dear I insist upon it

Chamb. Nay, pray, sir, don't be so positive; I can't stay, indeed.

Brush. You shall take one cup to our better acquaintance.

Chamb. I seldom drinks chocolate; and if I did, one has no satisfaction with such apprehensions about one. If my lord should awake, or the Swish gentleman should see one, or Madam Heidelberg should know of it, I should be frighted to death: besides, I have had my tea already this morning—I'm sure I hear my lord. [*Frightened.*

Brush. No, no, madam, don't flutter yourself—the moment my lord wakes, he rings his bell, which I answer sooner or later, as it suits my convenience.

Chamb. But should he come upon us without ringing?

Brush. I'll forgive him if he does. This key—[*Pointing to a range of phials*]—locks him up, till I please to let him out.

Chamb. Law, sir! that's potecary's stuff.

Brush. It is so: but without this he can no more get out of bed, than he can read without spectacles. [*Sips.*] What with qualms, age, rheumatisms, and a few surfeits in his youth, he must have a great deal of brushing, oiling, screwing, and winding up, to set him a-going for the day.

Chamb. [*Sips.*] That's prodigious indeed. [*Sips.*] My lord seems quite in a decay.

Brush. Yes, he's quite a spectacle, [*sips*] a mere corpse, till he is revived and refreshed from our little magazine here. When the restorative pills and cordial waters warm his stomach, and get into his head, vanity frisks in his heart, and then he sets up for the lover, the rake, and the fine gentleman.

Chamb. [*Sips.*] Poor gentleman! but should the Swish gentleman come upon us?   [*Frightened.*

Brush. Why then the English gentleman would be very angry. No foreigner must break in upon my privacy. [*Sips.*] But I can assure you Mr. Canton is otherwise employed—he is obliged to skim the cream of half a score newspapers for my lord's breakfast. Pray, madam, drink your cup peaceably. My lord's chocolate is remarkably good—he won't touch a drop, but what comes from Italy.

Chamb. [*Sipping.*] 'Tis very fine, indeed! [*sips*] and charmingly perfumed—it smells for all the world like our young ladies' dressing boxes.

Brush. You have an excellent taste, madam, and I must beg of you to accept of a few cakes for your own drinking, [*rise and advance*] and in return I desire nothing but to taste the perfume of your lips. [*Kissing her.*] A small return of favors, madam, will make, I hope, this country and retirement agreeable to both. [*He bows, she courtsies; return, and sit again.*] Your young ladies are fine girls, faith : [*sips*] tho', upon my soul, I am quite of my old lord's opinion about them, and were I inclined to matrimony, I should take the youngest.   [*Sips.*

Chamb. Miss Fanny's the most affablest and the most best natur'd creter !

Brush. And the eldest a little haughty or so—

Chamb. More haughtier and prouder than Saturn himself—but this I say quite confidential to you ; for one would not hurt a young lady's marriage, you know. [*Sips.*

Brush. By no means ; but you can't hurt it with us—we don't consider tempers—we wan't money, Mrs. Nancy ; give us enough of that, we'll abate you a great deal in other particulars.

Chamb. Bless me, here's somebody—[*bell rings*]—O ! 'tis my lord—Well, your servant, Mr. Brush—I'll clean the cups in the next room.

Brush. Do so—but never mind the bell—I shan't go this half hour. Will you drink tea with me in the afternoon ?

Chamb. Not for the world, Mr. Brush. I'll be here to set all things to rights—but I must not drink tea, indeed, and so your servant. [*Bell rings.—Exit, with tea-board,* L.

Brush. It is impossible to stupify one's self in the country for a week, without some little flirting with the Abigails : this is much the handsomest wench in the house, except the old citizen's youngest daughter, and I have not time enough to lay a plan for her. [*Bell rings.*] And now I'll go to my Lord, for I have nothing else to do.

[*Going.*

Enter CANTON, (R.) *with newspapers in his hand.*

Cant. Monsieur Brush—Maître Brush—my lor stirra yet ?

Brush. He has just rung his bell—I am going to him.

[*Exit, Brush.*

Cant. Dépêchez-vous donc. [*Puts on spectacles.*] I wish
de Deveil had all dese papiers—I forget as fast as I read
—De Advertise put out of my head de Gazette, de Gazette de Cronique, and so dey all go l'un après l'autre—I
must get some nouvelle for my lor, or he'ell be enragé
contre moi—Voyons ! [*Reads the Papers.*] Here is nothing
but Anti-Sejanus et advertise—

Enter MAID *with chocolate things.*

Vat you vant, child ?

Chamb. Only the chocolate things, sir.

Cant. Oh, ver well—dat is good girl—and very prit, too.
[*Exit Maid.*

Lord Ogl. [*Within.*] Canton, he, he, [*coughs*] Canton !

Cant. I come, my lor—vat shall I do ?—I have no news
—He will make great tintamarre !—

Lord Ogl. [*Within.*] Canton, I say, Canton ! Where
are you ?

Enter LORD OGLEBY, *leaning on* BRUSH.

Cant. Here, my lor; I ask pardon, my lor; I have not
finish de papiers—

Lord Ogl. Damn your pardon, and your papiers,—I
want you here, Canton.

Cant. Den I run, dat is all.   [*Shuffles along.*

[LORD OGLEBY *leans upon* CANTON *too, and comes
forward.*

Lord Ogl. You Swiss are the most unaccountable mix-
ture—you have the language and impertinence of the
French, with the laziness of Dutchmen.

Cant. 'Tis very true, my lor—I can't help—

Lord Ogl. [*Cries out*] O, Diavolo !

Cant. You are not in pain, I hope, my lor.

Lord Ogl. Indeed but I am, my lor.   That vulgar fellow, Sterling, with his city politeness, would force me
down his slope last night, to see a clay-coloured ditch,
which he calls a canal ; and what with the dew, and the
East wind, my hips and shoulders are absolutely screwed
to my body.

Cant. A littel véritable eau d'arquibusade vill set all to
right again.

[*My lord sits down in an easy-chair, and Brush gives
him chocolate.*

Lord Ogl. Where are the palsy drops, Brush ?
Brush. Here, my lord !   [*Pouring out.*
Lord Ogl. Quelle nouvelle avez-vous, Canton ?
Cant. A great deal of papier, but no news at all.
Lord Ogl. What ! nothing at all, you stupid fellow ?
Cant. Yes, my lor, I have a little advertise here vil give
you more plaisir den all de lyes about nothing at all.   La
voilá !   [*Puts on his spectacles.*
Lord Ogl. Come, read it, Canton, with good emphasis
and discretion.
Cant. I vil, my lor. [*Cant reads.*] Dere is no question,
but that the Cosmétique Royale vil utterlie take away all
heats, pimps, frecks, oder eruptions of de skin, and like-
wise de wrinque of old age, &c. &c.—A great deal more,
my lor—be sure to ask for de Cosmétique Royale, signed
by de Docteur own hand.   Dere is more raison for dis
caution dan good men vil tink.—Eh bien, my lor ?
Lord Ogl. Eh bien, Canton, will you purchase any ?
Cant. For you, my lor ?
Lord Ogl. For me, you old puppy ! for what ?
Cant. My lor ?
Lord Ogl. Do I want cosmetics ?
Cant. My lor ?
Lord Ogl. Look in my face.   Come, be sincere.   Does
it want the assistance of art ?
Cant. [*With his Spectacles.*] En vérité non.   'Tis very
smoose and brillian—but tote dat you might take a litle by
way of prevention.
Lord Ogl. You thought like an old fool, Monsieur, as
you generally do—The surfeit water, Brush ! [*Brush
pours out.*] What do you think, Brush of this family, we
are going to be connected with ?   Eh ?
Brush. Very well to marry in, my lord ; but it would
not do to live with.
Lord Ogl. You are right, Brush.   There is no washing
the blackamoor white—Mr. Sterling will never get rid of
Blackfriars, always taste of the Borachio ; and the poor
woman, his sister, is so busy and so notable to make one
welcome, that I have not yet got over her first reception ;
it almost amounted to suffocation ! I think the daughters
are tolerable—Where's my cephalic snuff ?
                              [*Brush gives him a box.*

Cant. Dey tink so of you, my lor, for dey look at no ting else, ma foi.

Lord Ogl. Did they? Why, I think they did a little—Where's my glass? [*Brush puts one on the table.*] The youngest is delectable. [*Takes snuff.*

Cant. O oui, my lor, very delect, inteed; she made doux yeux at you, my lor.

Lord Ogl. She was particular. The eldest, my nephew's lady, will be a most valuable wife; she has all the vulgar spirits of her father and aunt, happily blended with the termagant qualities of her deceased mother.—Some peppermint water, Brush!—How happy is it, Cant., for young ladies in general, that people of quality overlook every thing in a marriage contract but their fortune.

Cant. C'est bien heureux, et commode aussi.

Lord Ogl. Brush, give me that pamphlet by my bedside. [*Brush goes for it.*] Canton, do you wait in the ante-chamber, and let no one interrupt me till I call you.

Cant. Mush good may do your lordship! [*Exit,* R.

Lord Ogl. [*To Brush, who brings the pamphlet.*] And now, Brush, leave me a little to my studies.

[*Exit Brush,* L.

Lord Ogl. [*Alone.*] What can I possibly do among these women, here, with this confounded rheumatism? It is a most grievous enemy to gallantry and address. [*Rises.*] He! Courage, my lor! by heavens, I'm another creature. [*Hums and dances a little.*] It will do, faith. Bravo, my lor! These girls have absolutely inspired me. If they are for a game of romps—me voilà prêt! [*Sings and dances.*] Oh—that's an ugly twinge—but it's gone. I have rather too much of the lily this morning in my complexion; a faint tincture of the rose will give a delicate spirit to my eyes for the day. [*Unlocks a drawer at the bottom of the glass, and takes out rouge; while he's painting himself, a knocking at the door.*] Who's there? I won't be disturbed.

Cant. [*Without,* R.] My lor, my lor, here is Monsieur Sterling to pay his devoir to you this morn in your chambre.

Lord Ogl. [*Softly.*] What a fellow!—[*Aloud.*] I am extremely honoured by Mr. Sterling. Why don't you see him in, Monsieur? I wish he was at the bottom of his

c

stinking canal. [*Door opens.*] Oh, my dear Mr. Sterling you do me a great deal of honour.

Enter CANTON, STERLING, *and* LOVEWELL, R.

Ster. I hope, my lord, that your lordship slept well in the night—I believe there are no better beds in Europe than I have—I spare no pains to get 'em, nor money to buy them—His Majesty, God bless him, don't sleep upon a better out of his palace; and if I had said *in* too, I hope no treason, my lord.

Lord Ogl. Your beds are like everything else about you—incomparable. They not only make one rest well, but give one spirits, Mr. Sterling.

Ster. What say you, then, my lord, to another walk in the garden? You must see my water by daylight, and my walks, and my slopes, and my clumps, and my bridge, and my flowering trees, and my bed of Dutch tulips. Matters looked but dim last night, my lord; I feel the dew in my great toe—but I would put on a cut shoe, that I might be able to walk you about. I may be laid up to-morrow.

Lord Ogl. [*Aside.*] I pray heaven you may!

Ster. What say you, my lord?

Lord Ogl. I was saying, sir, that I was in hopes of seeing the young ladies at breakfast. Mr. Sterling, they are, in my mind, the finest tulips in this part of the world—he! he!

Cant. (L. C.) Bravissimo, my lor—ha! ha! ha!

Ster. They shall meet your lordship in the garden—we don't lose our walk for them; I'll take you a little round before breakfast, and a larger before dinner, and in the evening you shall go to the Grand Tower, as I call it—ha! ha! ha!

Lord Ogl. (C.) Not a foot, I hope, Mr. Sterling—consider your gout, my good friend. You'll certainly be laid by the heels for your politeness.

Cant. Ha! ha! ha! 'Tis admirable! en vérité!
                              [*Laughing very heartily.*

Ster. (R. C.) If my young man [*To Lovewell*] here would but laugh at my jokes, which he ought to do, as Mounseer does at yours, my lord, we should be all life and mirth.

Lord Ogl. Wha say you, Cant., will you take my

kinsman into your tuition? You have certainly the most companionable laugh I ever met with, and never out of tune—

Cant. But when your lordship is out of spirits.

Lord Ogl. Well said, Cant.; but here comes my nephew to play his part.

Enter Sir John Melvil, r.

Well, Sir John, what news from the island of Love? have you been sighing and serenading this morning?

Sir John. I am glad to see your lordship in such spirits this morning.

Lord Ogl. I'm sorry to see you so dull, sir. What poor things, Mr. Sterling, these *very* young fellows are! they make love with faces, as if they were burying the dead; though, indeed, a marriage sometimes may be properly called a burying of the living—eh, Mr. Sterling?

Ster. Not if they have enough to live upon, my lord—Ha! ha! ha!

Cant. Dat is all Monsieur Sterling tink of.

Sir John. [*Apart to Lovewell.*] Pr'ythee, Lovewell, come with me into the garden; I have something of consequence for you, and I must communicate it directly.

Lov. We'll go together.—If your lordship and Mr. Sterling please, we'll prepare the ladies to attend you in the garden.   [*Exeunt Sir John and Lovewell, r.*

Ster. My girls are always ready; I make 'em rise soon and to bed early; their husbands shall have 'em with good constitutions and good fortunes, if they have nothing else, my lord.

Lord Ogl. Fine things, Mr. Sterling!

Ster. Fine things, indeed, my lord! Ah, my lord, had not you run off your speed in your youth, you had not been so crippled in your age, my lord.

Lord Ogl. Very pleasant.   [*Half laughing.*

Ster. Here's Mounseer, now, I suppose, is pretty near your lordship's standing; but having little to eat, and little to spend, in his own country, he'll wear three of your lordship out—eating and drinking kills us all.

Lord Ogl. Very pleasant, I protest.—[*Aside.*] What a vulgar dog!

Cant. My lor so old as me? He is chicken to me, and look like a boy to pauvre me.

Ster. Ha! ha! ha! Well said, Mounseer—keep to that,
and you'll live in any country of the world—Ha! ha! ha!
But, my lord, I will wait upon you in the garden; we
have but a little time to breakfast—I'll go for my hat and
cane, fetch a little walk with you, my lord, and then for
the hot rolls an l butter! [*Exit*, R.

Lord Ogl. I shall attend you with pleasure. Hot rolls
and butter in July! I sweat with the thoughts of it. What
a strange beast it is!

Cant. C'est un barbare.

Lord Ogl. He is a vulgar dog, and if there was not so
much money in the family, which I can't do without, l
would leave him and his hot rolls and butter directly.
Come along, Monsieur! [*Exeunt Lord Ogl. and Cant.*, R.

SCENE II.—*A Garden.*

Enter SIR JOHN MELVIL *and* LOVEWELL, L.

Lov. In my room this morning? Impossible.

Sir John. Before five this morning, I promise you.

Lov. On what occasion?

Sir John. I was so anxious to disclose my mind to you,
that I could not sleep in my bed—but I found that you
could not sleep neither—the bird was flown, and the nest
long since cold. Where was you, Lovewell?

Lov. Pooh! prithee! ridiculous!

Sir John. Come, now, which was it? Miss Sterling's
maid! a pretty little rogue! or Miss Fanny's Abigail? a
sweet soul too—or—

Lov. Nay, nay, leave trifling, and tell me your business.

Sir John. Well, but where was you, Lovewell?

Lov. Walking—writing—what signifies where I was?

Sir John. Walking! yes, I dare say. It rained as hard
as it could pour. Sweet refreshing showers to walk in!
No, no, Lovewell. Now would I give twenty pounds to
know which of the maids—

Lov. But your business—your business, Sir John!

Sir John. Let me a little into the secrets of the family

Lov. Psha!

Sir John. [*Aside.*] Poor Lovewell, he can't bear it, I
see.—[*Aloud.*] She charged you not to kiss and tell—eh,

Lovewell ?   However, though you will not honour me
with your confidence, I'll venture to trust you with mine.
What do you think of Miss Sterling ?

Lov. What do I think of Miss Sterling ?

Sir John. Ay, what d'ye think of her ?

Lov. An odd question ! But I think her a smart, lively
girl, full of mirth and sprightliness.

Sir John. All mischief and malice, I doubt not.

Lov. How ?

Sir John. But her person, what d'ye think of that ?

' *Lov.* Pretty and agreeable.

Sir John. An awkward creature.

Lov. What is the meaning of all this ?

Sir John. I'll tell you. You must know, Lovewell, that
notwithstanding all appearances—[*Seeing Lord Ogleby
&c.*]—We are interrupted : when they are gone, I'll explain.

Enter Lord Ogleby, Sterling, Mrs. Heidelberg, Miss
Sterling, *and* Fanny, l. s. e.

Lord Ogl. (c.) Great improvements, indeed, Mr. Ster-
ling! wonderful improvements! The Four Seasons in
Lead, the Flying Mercury, and the basin with Neptune
in the middle, are all in the very extreme of fine taste.
You have as many rich figures as the man at Hyde Park
Corner.

Ster. (r. c.) The chief pleasure of a country house is
to make improvements, you know, my lord. I spare no
expense, not I. This is quite another guess sort of a place
than it was when I first took it, my lord. We were surrounded with trees. I cut down above fifty to make the
lawn before the house, and let in the wind and the sun—
smack-smooth—as you see. Then I made a green-house
out of the old laundry, and turned the brew-house into
a pinery. The high octagon summer-house, you see yonder, is raised on the mast of a ship, given me by an East
India captain, who has turned many a thousand of my
money. It commands the whole road. All the coaches,
and chariots, and chaises pass and repass under your eye.
I'll mount you up there in the afternoon, my lord. 'Tis
the pleasantest place in the world to take a pipe and a
bottle ; and so you shall say, my lord.

Lord Ogl. Ay, or a bowl of punch, or a can of flip, Mr.

Sterling; for it looks like a cabin in the air. If flying chairs were in use, the captain might make a voyage to the Indies in it still, if he had but a fair wind.

Cant. Ha! ha! ha! ha!

Mrs. Hei. (L. C.) My brother's a little comical in his ideas, my lord—but you'll excuse him. I have a little Gothic dairy, fitted up entirely in my own taste. In the evening I shall hope for the honour of your lordship's company to take a dish of tea there, or a syllabub warm from the cow.

Lord Ogl. I have every moment a fresh opportunity of admiring the elegance of Mrs. Heidelberg—the very flower of delicacy, and cream of politeness.

Mrs. Hei. Oh, my lord!   } *[Leering at each other.*
Lord Ogl. Oh, madam!   }

Ster. How d'ye like these close walks, my lord?

Lord Ogl. A most excellent serpentine! It forms a perfect maze, and winds like a true lover's knot.

Ster. Ay, here's none of your straight lines here—but all taste—zig-zag—crinkum-crankum—in and out—right and left—to and again—twisting and turning like a worm, my lord!

Lord Ogl. Admirably laid out, indeed, Mr. Sterling! one can hardly see an inch beyond one's nose anywhere in these walks. You are a most excellent economist of your land, and make a little go a great way. It lies together in as small parcels as if it was placed in pots out at your window in Gracechurch street.

Cant. Ha! ha! ha! ha!

Lord Ogl. What d'ye laugh at, Canton?

Cant. Ah! que cette similitude est drole! So clever what you say, my lor!

Lord Ogl. [*To Fanny.*] You seem mightily engaged, madam. What are those pretty hands so busily employed about?

Fanny. Only making up a nosegay, my lord. Will your lordship do me the honour of accepting it?
                                        [*Presenting it.*

Lord Ogl. I'll wear it next my heart, madam! [*Apart.*] I see, the young creature doats on me!

Miss Ster. Lord, sister! you've loaded his lordship with a bunch of flowers as big as the cook or the nurse carry

to town on Monday morning for a beau-pot. Will your
lordship give me leave to present you with this rose and
a sprig of sweet-briar?

Lord Ogl. The truest emblems of yourself, madam! all
sweetness and poignancy.—[*Apart.*] A little jealous, poor
soul!

Ster. Now, my lord, if you please, I'll carry you to see
my ruins.

Mrs. Hei. You'll absolutely fatigue his lordship with
over-walking, brother.

Lord Ogl. Not at all, madam. We're in the garden of
Eden, you know; in the region of perpetual spring, youth,
and beauty.   [*Leering at the women, who stand,* l.

Mrs. Hei. [*Apart.*] Quite the man of qualaty, I pertest.

Cant. Take a my arm, my lor. [*Lord O. leans on him.*

Ster. I'll only show his lordship my ruins, and the cas-
cade, and the Chinese bridge, and then we'll go in to breakfast.

Lord Ogl. Ruins, did you say, Mr. Sterling?

Ster. Ay, ruins, my lord! and they are reckoned very
fine ones, too. You would think them ready to tumble on
your head. It has just cost me a hundred and fifty pounds
to put my ruins in thorough repair. This way, if your
lordship pleases.

Lord Ogl. [*Going, stops.*] What steeple's that we see
yonder?—the parish church, I suppose.

Ster. Ha! ha ha! that's admirable. It is no church
at all, my lord! it is a spire that I have built against a
tree, a field or two off, to terminate the prospect. One
must always have a church, or an obelisk, or something
to terminate the prospect, you know. That's a rule in
taste, my lord!

Lord Ogl. (c.) Very ingenious, indeed! For my part,
I desire no finer prospect than I see before me. [*Leering
at the women.*] Simple, yet varied: bounded, yet exten-
sive.—Get away, Canton! [*Pushing away Canton.*] I want
no assistance—I'll walk with the ladies.

Ster. This way, my lord!

Lord Ogl. Lead on, sir!—We young folks will follow
you. Madam!—Miss Sterling!—Miss Fanny!—I attend
you.   [*Exit after Sterling, gallanting the ladies.*

Cant. [*Following.*] He is cock o' de game, ma foi!

[*Exit.—Sir John Melvil and Lovewell come forward.*

Sir John. At length, thank heaven, I have an opportunity to unbosom.—I know you are faithful, Lovewell, and flatter myself you would rejoice to serve me.

Lov. Be assured, you may depend on me.

Sir John. You must know, then, notwithstanding all appearances, that this treaty of marriage between Miss Sterling and me will come to nothing.

Lor. How!

Sir John. It will be no match, Lovewell.

Lov. No match?

Sir John. No.

Lov. You amaze me. What should prevent it?

Sir John. I.

Lov. You! wherefore?

Sir John. I don't like her.

Lov. Very plain indeed! I never supposed that you was extremely devoted to her from inclination, but thought you always considered it as a matter of convenience, rather than affection.

Sir John. Very true. I came into the family without any impression on my mind—with an unimpassioned indifference, ready to receive one woman as well as another. I looked upon love, serious, sober love, as a chimera, and marriage as a thing of course, as you know most people do. But I, who was lately so great an infidel in love, am now one of its sincerest votaries. In short, my defection from Miss Sterling proceeds from the violence of my attachment to another.

Lov. (R. C.) Another! So, so! here will be fine work. And pray, who is she?

Sir John. (C.) Who is she? who can she be, but Fanny, the tender, amiable, engaging Fanny?

Lov. Fanny! What Fanny?

Sir John. Fanny Sterling; her sister. Is she not an angel, Lovewell?

Lov. Her sister? Confusion!—You must not think of it, Sir John.

Sir John. Not think of it? I can think of nothing else. Nay, tell me, Lovewell! was it possible for me to be indulged in a perpetual intercourse with two such objects as Fanny and her sister, and not find my heart led by insensible attraction towards her? You seem confounded! Why don't you answer me?

Lov. Indeed, Sir John, this event gives me infinite concern.

Sir John. Why so? Is she not an angel, Lovewell?

Lov. I foresee that it must produce the worst consequences. Consider the confusion it must unavoidably create. Let me persuade you to drop these thoughts in time.

Sir John. Never—never, Lovewell!

Lov. You have gone too far to recede. A negociation, so nearly concluded, cannot be broken off with any grace. The lawyers, you know, are hourly expected; the preliminaries almost finally settled between Lord Ogleby and Mr. Sterling; and Miss Sterling herself ready to receive you as a husband.

Sir John. Why, the banns have been published, and nobody has forbidden them, 'tis true. But you know either of the parties may change their minds even after they enter the church.

Lov. You think too lightly of this matter. To carry your addresses so far—and then to desert her—and for her sister, too! It will be such an affront to the family, that they can never put up with it.

Sir John. I don't think so: for as to my transferring my passion from her to her sister, so much the better! for then, you know, I don't carry my affection out of the family.

Lov. Nay, but prythee, be serious, and think better of it.

Sir John. I have thought better of it already, you see. Tell me honestly, Lovewell, can you blame me? Is there any comparison between them?

Lov. As to that, now—Why, that—is just—just as it may strike different people. There are many admirers of Miss Sterling's vivacity.

Sir John. Vivacity! a medley of Cheapside pertness, and Whitechapel pride. No, no, if I do go so far into the city for a wedding-dinner, it shall be upon turtle, at least.

Lov. But I see no probability of success; for granting that Mr. Sterling would have consented to it at first, he cannot listen to it now. Why did not you break this affair to the family before?

Sir John. Under such embarrassed circumstances as I have been, can you wonder at my irresolution or perplexity? Nothing but despair, the fear of losing my dear Fanny, could bring me to a declaration even now; and yet I think I know Mr. Sterling so well, that strange as my proposal may appear, if I can make it advantageous to him as a money transaction, as I am sure I can, he will certainly come into it.

Lov. But even suppose he should, which I very much doubt, I don't think Fanny herself would listen to your addresses.

Sir John. You are deceived a little in that particular.

Lov. You'll find I am in the right.

Sir John. I have some little reason to think otherwise.

Lov. You have not declared your passion to her already?

Sir John. Yes, I have.

Lov. Indeed!—And—and—how did she receive it?

Sir John. I think it is not very easy for me to make my addresses to any woman, without receiving some little encouragement.

Lov. Encouragement! did she give you any encouragement?

Sir John. I don't know what you call encouragement—but she blushed—and cried—and desired me not to think of it any more—upon which I pressed her hand—kissed it—swore she was an angel—and I could see it tickled her to the soul.

Lov. And did she express no surprise at your declaration?

Sir John. Why, faith, to say the truth, she was a little surprised—and she got away from me too, before I could thoroughly explain myself. If I should not meet with an opportunity of speaking to her, I must get you to deliver a letter for me.

Lov. I! a letter!—I had rather have nothing—

Sir John. Nay, you promised me your assistance—and I am sure you cannot scruple to make yourself useful on such an occasion—You may, without suspicion, acquaint her verbally of my determined affection for her, and that I am resolved to ask her father's consent.

Lov. As to that, I—your commands, you know—that is, if she—Indeed, Sir John, I think you are in the wrong.

Sir John. Well—well—that's my concern—Ha! there she goes, by heaven! along that walk, yonder, d'ye see? I'll go to her immediately.

Lov. You are too precipitate. Consider what you are doing!

Sir John. I would not lose this opportunity for the universe.

Lov. Nay, pray don't go! Your violence and eagerness may overcome her spirits. The shock will be too much for her.   [*Detaining him.*

Sir John. Nothing shall prevent me. Ha! now she turns into another walk—let me go! [*Breaks from him.*] I shall lose her. [*Going, turns back.*] Be sure now to keep out of the way! If you interrupt us, I shall never forgive you.

                                      [*Exit, hastily,* R.

Lov. (c) 'Sdeath! I can't bear this. In love with my wife! acquaint me with his passion for her! make his addresses before my face! I shall break out before my time—This was the meaning of Fanny's uneasiness. She could not encourage him—I am sure she could not—Ha! they are turning into the walk, and coming this way. Shall I leave the place?—Leave him to solicit my wife! I can't submit to it—They come nearer and nearer—If I stay, it will look suspicious—It may betray us and incense him—They are here—I must go—I am the most unfortunate fellow in the world.   [*Exit,* L.

Enter FANNY, *followed by* SIR JOHN, R.

Fanny. (c.) Leave me, Sir John, I beseech you, leave me; nay, why will you persist to follow me with idle solicitations, which are an affront to my character, and an injury to your own honour?

Sir John. (R. c.) I know your delicacy, and tremble to offend it; but let the urgency of the occasion be my excuse! Consider, madam, that the future happiness of my life depends on my present application to you! consider that this day must determine my fate; and these are perhaps the only moments left me to incline you to warrant my passion, and to intreat you not to oppose the proposals I mean to open to your father.

Fanny. For shame, for shame, Sir John! Think of your previous engagements! Think of your own situation,

at d think of mine! What have you discovered in my conduct that might encourage you to so bold a declaration? I
am shocked that you might venture to say so much, and
blush that I should even dare to give it a hearing.—Let
me be gone!

Sir John. Nay, stay madam, but one moment—Your
sensibility is too great. Engagements! what engagements
have been pretended on either side more than those of family convenience? I went on in the trammels of matrimo-
nial negociation with a blind submission to your father and
Lord Ogleby; but my heart soon claimed a right to be
consulted. It has devoted itself to you, and obliges me
to plead earnestly for the same tender interest in yours.

Fanny. Have a care, Sir John! do not mistake a de-
praved will for a virtuous inclination. By these common
pretences of the heart, half our sex are made fools, and a
greater part of yours despise them for it.

Sir John. Affection, you will allow, is involuntary. We
cannot always direct it to the object on which it should fix
—But when it is once inviolably attached, inviolably as mine
is to you, it often creates reciprocal affection. When I
last urged you on this subject, you heard me with more
temper, and I hoped with some compassion.

Fanny. You deceived yourself. If I forbore to exert a
proper spirit; nay, if I did not even express the quickest
resentment of your behaviour, it was only in consideration
of that respect I wish to pay you, in honour to my sister:
and be assured, sir, woman as I am, that my vanity could
reap no pleasure from a triumph that must result from the
blackest treachery to her.   [*Going.*

Sir John. One word, and I have done. [*Stopping her.*]
Your impatience and anxiety, and the urgency of the occasion, oblige me to be brief and explicit with you—I ap-
peal therefore from your delicacy to your justice. Your
sister, I verily believe, neither entertains any real affection
for me, or tenderness for you. Your father, I am inclined
to think, is not much concerned by means of which of his
daughters the families are united. Now, as they cannot,
shall not be connected, otherwise than by my union with you,
why will you, from a false delicacy, oppose a measure so
conducive to my happiness, and, I hope, your own? I love
you, most passionately an I sincerely love you—and I hope

to propose terms agreeable to Mr. Sterling:—If then you
don't absolutely loath, abhor, and scorn me—if there is no
other happier man—

Fanny. Hear me, sir, hear my final determination.
Were my father and sister as insensible as you are pleased
to represent them ;—were my heart for ever to remain
disengaged to any other—I could not listen to your proposals. What ! you on the very eve of a marriage with my
sister ; I living under the same roof with her, bound not
only by the laws of friendship and hospitality, but even the
ties of blood, to contribute to her happiness—and not to
conspire against her peace—the peace of a whole family—
and that my own too !—Away, away, Sir John !—At such
a time, and in such circumstances, your addresses only in-
spire me with horror—Nay, you must detain me no longer
—I will go.   [*Going, L.*

Sir John. Do not leave me in absolute despair !—Give
me a glimpse of hope !   [*Falling on his knees, L.*

Fanny. I cannot. Pray, Sir John ! [*Struggling to go.*

Sir John. Shall this hand be given to another ? [*Kissing
her hand.*] No—I cannot endure it—My whole soul is
yours, and the whole happiness of my life is in your power.

Enter Miss Sterling, R. U. E.

Fanny. (L.) Ha ! My sister is here. Rise, for shame,
Sir John !

Sir John. Miss Sterling!   [*Rising.*

Miss Ster. (R.) I beg pardon, sir ! You'll excuse me,
madam ! I have broke in upon you a little inopportunely,
I believe—but I did not mean to interrupt you—I only
came, sir, to let you know that breakfast waits, if you have
finished your morning's devotions.

Sir John. (R.) I am very sensible, Miss Sterling, that
this may appear particular, but—

Miss Ster. (C.) O dear, Sir John, don't put yourself to
the trouble of an apology. The thing explains itself.

Sir John. It will soon, madam ! In the mean time I can
only assure you of my profound respect and esteem for
you, and make no doubt of convincing Mr. Sterling of the
honour and integrity of my intentions. And—and—your
humble servant, madam !   [*Exit, in confusion, R.*

Miss Ster. Respect ?—Insolence !—Esteem ?—Very fine

D

truly! And you, madam! my sweet, delicate, innocent, sentimental sister! will you convince my papa, too, of the integrity of your intentions?

Fanny. Do not upbraid me, my dear sister! Indeed I don't deserve it. Believe me, you can't be more offended at his behaviour than I am, and I am sure it cannot make you half so miserable.

Miss Ster. Make me miserable! You are mightily deceived, madam! It gives me no sort of uneasiness, I assure you.—A base fellow!—As for you, miss! the pretended softness of your disposition, your artful good-nature, never imposed upon me. I always knew you to be sly, and envious, and deceitful.

Fanny. Indeed, you wrong me.

Miss Ster. Oh, you are all goodness, to be sure!—Did not I find him on his knees before you? Did not I see him kiss your sweet hand? Did not I hear his protestations? Was not I a witness of your dissembled modesty?—No, no, my dear! don't imagine that you can make a fool of your elder sister so easily.

Fanny. Sir John, I own, is to blame; but I am above the thoughts of doing you the least injury.

Miss Ster. We shall try that, madam!—I hope, miss, you'll be able to give a better account to my papa and my aunt—for they shall both know of this matter, I promise you.   [*Exit*, R.

Fanny. [*Alone.*] How unhappy I am! my distresses multiply upon me. Mr. Lovewell must now become acquainted with Sir John's behaviour to me—and in a manner that may add to his uneasiness. My father, instead of being disposed by fortunate circumstances to forgive any transgressions, will be previously incensed against me. My sister and my aunt will become irreconcilably my enemies, and rejoice in my disgrace. Yet, at all events, I am determined on a discovery. I dread it, and am resolved to hasten it. It is surrounded with more horrors every instant, as it appears every instant more necessary.   [*Exit*, R.

END OF ACT II.

ACT III.

Scene I.—*A Hall.*

Enter, ʟ.., *a* Servant, *leading in* Sergeant Flower, *and* Counsellors Traverse *and* Trueman—*all booted.*

Serv. This way, if you please, gentlemen! my master is at breakfast with the family at present—but I'll let him know, and he'll wait on you immediately.

Flower. Mighty well, young man, mighty well.

Serv. Please to favour me with your names, gentlemen.

Flower. Let Mr. Sterling know, that Mr. Sergeant Flower, and two other gentlemen of the bar, are come to wait on him, according to his appointment.

Serv. I will, sir.   [*Going*, ʟ..

Flower. And harkee, young man. [*Servant returns.*] Desire my servant—Mr. Sergeant Flower's servant—to bring in my green and gold saddle-cloth and pistols, and lay them down here in the hall with my portmanteau.

Serv. I will, sir.   [*Exit*, ʟ.

Flower. Well, gentlemen! the settling these marriage articles falls conveniently enough, almost just on the eve of the circuits. Let me see—the Home, the Midland, and Western; ay, we can all cross the country well enough to our several destinations. Traverse, when do you begin at Hertford?

Traverse. The day after to-morrow.

Flower. That is commission-day with us at Warwick too. But my clerk has retainers for every cause in the paper, so it will be time enough if I am there the next morning. Besides, I have about half a dozen cases that have lain by me ever since the spring assizes, and I must tack opinions to them before I see my country clients again. So I will take the evening before me—and then *currente calamo,* as I say—eh, Traverse?

Traverse. True, Mr. Sergeant—and the easiest thing in the world too—for those country attorneys are such ignorant dogs, that in case of the devise of an estate to A, and his heirs for ever, they'll make a query, whether he takes in fee or in tail.

Flower. Do you expect to have much to do on the home circuit these assizes ?

Traverse. Not much *nisi prius* business, but a good deal on the crown side, I believe. The gaols are brim full—and some of the felons in good circumstances, and likely to be tolerable clients. Let me see ; I am engaged for three highway robberies, three murders, one forgery, and half a dozen larcenies, at Kingston.

Flower. A pretty decent gaol delivery ! Do you expect to bring off Darking, for the robbery on Putney-Common ? Can you make out your *alibi?*

Traverse. Oh, no ! the crown witnesses are sure to prove our indentity. We shall certainly be hanged : but that don't signify. But Mr. Sergeant, have you much to do ? —any remarkable cause on the Midland this circuit ?

Flower. Nothing very remarkable—except two rapes, and Rider and Western at Nottingham, for *crim con ;*— but, on the whole, I believe a good deal of business. Our associate tells me, there are above thirty *venires* for Warwick.

Traverse. Pray, Mr. Sergeant, are you concerned in Jones and Thomas, at Lincoln ?

Flower. I am—for the plaintiff.

Traverse. And what do you think on't ?

Flower. A nonsuit.

Traverse. I thought so.

Flower. Oh, no manner of doubt on't—*luce clarius*—we have no right in us—we have but one chance.

Traverse. What's that ?

Flower. Why, my Lord Chief does not go the circuit this time, and my brother Puzzle being in the commission, the cause will come on before him.

Trueman. Ay, that may do, indeed, if you can but throw dust in the eyes of the defendant's counsel.

Flower. True.—Mr. Trueman, I think you are concerned for Lord Ogleby in this affair.   [*To Trueman.*

Trueman. I am, sir—I have the honour to be related to his lordship, and hold some courts for him in Somersetshire—go the Western circuit—and attend the sessions at Exeter, merely because his lordship's interests and property lie in that part of the kingdom.

Flower. Ha ! and pray, Mr. Trueman, how long have you been called to the bar ?

Trueman. About nine years and three quarters.

Flower. Ha! I don't know that I ever had the pleasure of seeing you before. I wish you success, young gentleman.

Enter STERLING, R.

Ster. Oh, Mr. Sergeant Flower, I am glad to see you. Your servant, Mr. Sergeant! gentlemen, your servant! Well, are all matters concluded? has that snail-paced conveyancer, old Ferret, of Gray's Inn, settled the articles at last? Do you approve of what he has done? Will his tackle hold, tight and strong?—Eh, master Sergeant?

Flower. My friend Ferret's slow and sure, sir. But then *serius aut citius*, as we say, sooner or later, Mr. Sterling, he is sure to put his business out of hand as he should do. My clerk has brought the writing, and all other instruments along with him, and the settlement is, I believe, as good a settlement as any settlement on the face of the earth.

Ster. But that damned mortgage of 60,000*l.* There don't appear to be any other incumbrances, I hope?

Traverse. I can answer for that, sir; and that will be cleared off immediately on the payment of the first part of Miss Sterling's portion. You agree, on your part, to come down with 80,000*l.*

Ster. Down on the nail. Ay, ay, my money is ready to-morrow, if he pleases: he shall have it in India-bonds, or notes, or how he chooses. Your lords and your dukes, and your people at the court-end of the town, stick at payments sometimes—debts unpaid, no credit lost with them—but no fear of us substantial fellows—eh, Mr. Sergeant?

Flower. Sir John having last term, according to agreement, levied a fine, and suffered a recovery, has hitherto cut off the entail of the Ogleby estate for the better effecting the purposes of the present intended marriage; on which above-mentioned Ogleby estate, a jointure of 2000*l.* per annum is secured to your eldest daughter, now Elizabeth Sterling, spinster, and the whole estate, after the death of the aforesaid earl, descends to the heirs male of Sir John Melvil, on the body of the aforesaid Elizabeth Sterling lawfully to be begotten.

Traverse. Very true—and Sir John is to be put in immaliate possession of as much of his lordship's Somerset-shire estate, as lies in the manors of Hogmore and Cran-ford, amounting to between two and three thousand per annum, and at the death of Mr. Sterling, a further sum of seventy thousand—

Enter SIR JOHN MELVIL. R.

Ster. Ah, Sir John! Here we are hard at it—paving the road to matrimony—first the lawyers, then comes the doctor—let us but dispatch the long robe, we shall soon get pudding-sleeves to work, I warrant you.

Sir John. I am sorry to interrupt you, sir—but I hope that both you and these gentlemen will excuse me—hav-ing something particular for your private ear, I took the liberty of following you, and beg you will oblige me with an audience immediately.

Ster. Ay, with all my heart!—Gentlemen, Mr. Sergeant, you'll excuse it—business must be done, you know. The writings will keep cold till to-morrow morning.

Flower. I must be at Warwick, Mr. Sterling, the day after.

Ster. Nay, nay, I sha'n't part with you to-night, gentle-men, I promise you. My house is very full, but I have beds for you all, beds for your servants, and stabling for all your horses. Will you take a turn in the garden, and view some of my improvements before dinner? Or will you amuse yourselves on the green, with a game of bowls and a cool tankard? My servants shall attend you. Do you choose any other refreshment? Call for what you please; do as you please; make yourselves quite at home, I beg of you. Here, Thomas! Harry! William! wait on these gentlemen!—[*Follows the Lawyers out, 1.., bawl-ing and talking, and then returns to Sir John.*] And now, sir, I am entirely at your service. What are your com-mands with me, Sir John?

Sir John. After having carried the negociation between our families to so great a length, after having assented so readily to all your proposals, as well as received so many instances of your cheerful compliance with the demands made on our part, I am extremely concerned, Mr. Sterling, to be the involuntary cause of any uneasiness.

Ster. Uneasiness! What uneasiness? Where business

is transacted as it ought to be, and the parties understand one another, there can be no uneasiness. You agree, on such and such conditions, to receive my daughter for a wife ; on the same conditions, I agree to receive you as a son-in-law ; and as to all the rest, it follows of course, you know, as regularly as the payment of a bill after acceptance.

Sir John. Pardon me, sir, more uneasiness has arisen than you are aware of. I am myself, at this instant, in a state of inexpressible embarrassment ; Miss Sterling, I know, is extremely disconcerted, too ; and unless you will oblige me with the assistance of your friendship, I foresee the speedy progress of discontent and animosity through the whole family.

Ster. What the deuce is all this ? I don't understand a single syllable.

Sir John. In one word, then—it will be absolutely impossible for me to fulfil my engagements in regard to Miss Sterling.

Ster. How, Sir John ! Do you mean to put an affront upon my family ? What ! refuse to—

Sir John. Be assured, sir, that I neither mean to affront, nor forsake your family. My only fear is, that you should desert me ; for the whole happiness of my life depends on my being connected with your family by the nearest and tenderest ties in the world.

Ster. Why, did not you tell me, but a moment ago, that it was absolutely impossible for you to marry my daughter?

Sir John. True. But you have another daughter, sir—

Ster. Well ?

Sir John. Who has obtained the most absolute dominion over my heart. I have already declared my passion to her; nay, Miss Sterling herself is also apprised of it ; and if you will but give a sanction to my present addresses, the uncommon merit of Miss Sterling will no doubt recommend her to a person of equal, if not superior rank to myself, and our families may still be allied by my union with Miss Fanny.

Ster. Mighty fine, truly ! Why, what the plague do you make of us, Sir John ? Do you come to market for my daughter, like servants at a statute-fair ? Do you think that I will suffer you, or any man in the world, to come

into my house, like the Grand Signior, and throw the handkerchief first to one, and then to t'other, just as he pleases?
Do you think I drive a kind of African slave-trade with
them; and—

Sir John. A moment's patience, sir! Nothing but the
excess of my passion for Miss Fanny should have induced
me to take any step that had the least appearance of dis-
respect to any part of your family; and even now I am
desirous to atone for my transgression, by making the most
adequate compensation that lies in my power.

Ster. Compensation! what compensation can you possibly make in such a case as this, Sir John?

Sir John. Come, come, Mr. Sterling; I know you to
be a man of sense, a man of business, a man of the
world. I'll deal frankly with you; and you shall see that
I don't desire a change of measures for my own gratifi-
cation, without endeavouring to make it advantageous to
you.

Ster. What advantage can your inconstancy be to me,
Sir John?

Sir John. I'll tell you, sir. You know that by the articles at present subsisting between us, on the day of my
marriage with Miss Sterling, you agree to pay down the
gross sum of eighty thousand pounds.

Ster. Well!

Sir John. Now if you will but consent to my waiving
that marriage—

Ster. I agree to your waiving that marriage? Impossible, Sir John!

Sir John. I hope not, sir; as on my part, I will agree
to waive my right to thirty thousand pounds of the fortune I was to receive with her.

Ster. Thirty thousand, d'ye say?

Sir John. Yes, sir; and accept of Miss Fanny with fifty thousand, instead of fourscore.

Ster. Fifty thousand—   [*Pausing.*

Sir John. Instead of fourscore.

Ster. Why—why—there may be something in that. Let
me see—Fanny with fifty thousand, instead of Betsy
with fourscore. But how can this be, Sir John? For
you know I am to pay this money into the hands of my
Lord Ogleby; who, I believe—between you and me, Sir

John—is not overstocked with ready money at present ; and threescore thousand of it, you know, is to go to pay off the present incumbrances on the estate, Sir John.

Sir John. That objection is easily obviated. Ten of the twenty thousand, which would remain as a surplus of the fourscore, after paying off the mortgage, was intended by his lordship for my use, that we might set off with some little eclat on our marriage ; and the other ten for his own. Ten thousand pounds, therefore, I shall be able to pay you immediately ; and for the remaining twenty thousand, you shall have a mortgage on that part of the estate which is to be made over to me, with whatever security you shall require for the regular payment of the interest, till the principal is duly discharged.

Ster. Why—to do you justice, Sir John, there is something fair and open in your proposal ; and since I find you do not mean to put an affront upon the family—

Sir John. Nothing was ever farther from my thoughts, Mr. Sterling. And after all, the whole affair is nothing extraordinary—such things happen every day—and as the world has only heard generally of a treaty between the families, when this marriage takes place, nobody will be the wiser, if we have but discretion enough to keep our own counsel.

Ster. True, true ; and since you only transfer from one girl to the other, it is no more than transferring so much stock, you know.

Sir John. The very thing !

Ster. Odso ! I had quite forgot. We are reckoning without our host here. There is another difficulty—

Sir John. You alarm me. What can that be ?

Ster. I can't stir a step in this business without consulting my sister Heidelberg. The family has very great expectations from her, and we must not give her any offence.

Sir John. But if you come into this measure, surely she will be so kind as to consent—

Ster. I don't know that—Betsy is her darling, and I can't tell how far she may resent any slight that seems to be offered to her favourite niece. However, I'll do the best I can for you. You shall go and break the matter to her first, and by the time I may suppose that your rhe-

toric has prevailed on her to listen to reason, I will step in
to reinforce your arguments.

Sir John. I'll fly to her immediately ; you promise me
your assistance ?

Ster. I do.

Sir John. Ten thousand thanks for it ! and now success
attend me !   [*Going,* R.

Ster. (L.) Harkee, Sir John ! [*Sir John returns.*] Not
a word of the thirty thousand to my sister, Sir John.

Sir John. Oh, I am dumb—I am dumb, sir.   [*Going.*

Ster. You remember it is thirty thousand.

Sir John. To be sure, I do.

Ster. But, Sir John!—one thing more. [*Sir John returns.*] My lord must know nothing of this stroke of friendship between us.

Sir John. Not for the world. Let me alone! let me
alone !   [*Offering to go.*

Ster. [*Holding him.*] And when every thing is agreed,
we must give each other a bond to be held fast to the bargain.

Sir John. To be sure. A bond by all means ! a bond,
or whatever you please.   [*Exit hastily,* R.

Ster. [*Alone.*] I should have thought of more conditions—he's in a humour to give me every thing. [*Exit,* L.

SCENE II.—*Another Apartment.*

Enter MRS. HEIDELBERG *and* MISS STERLING, L.

Miss Ster. This is your gentle-looking, soft-speaking,
sweet-smiling, affable Miss Fanny for you!

Mrs. Hei. My Miss Fanny ! I disclaim her. With all
her arts she never could insinuate herself into my good
graces—and yet she has a way with her, that deceives
man, woman, and child, except you and me, niece.

Miss Ster. Oh, ay ; she wants nothing but a crook in
her hand, and a lamb under her arm, to be a perfect pic-
ture of innocence and simplicity.

Mrs. Hei. Just as I was drawn at Amsterdam, when I
went over to visit my husband's relations.

Miss Ster. And then she's so mighty good to servants
—" Pray, John, do this—pray, Tom, do that—thank you,
Jenny"—and then so humble to her relations—" To be

sure, papa !—as my aunt pleases—my sister knows best."
But with all her demureness and humility, she has no objection to be Lady Melvil, it seems, nor to any wickedness that can make her so.

Mrs. Hei. She Lady Melvil ? Compose yourself, niece !
I'll ladyship her indeed ! a little creppin, cantin—she
shan't be the better for a farden of my money. But tell
me, child, how does this intriguing with Sir John corres-
pond with her partiality to Lovewell ? I don't see a con-
catunation here.

Miss Ster. There I was deceived, madam. I took all
their whisperings and stealing into corners to be the mere
attraction of vulgar minds : but, behold ! their private
meetings were not to contrive their own insipid happiness, but to conspire against mine. But I know whence
proceeds Mr. Lovewell's resentment to me. I could not
stoop to be familiar with my father's clerk, and so I have
lost his interest.

Mrs. Hei. My spurrit to a T.—my dear child ! [*Kisses
her.*] Mr. Heidelberg lost his election for member of parliament, because I would not demean myself to be slob-
bered about by drunken shoemakers, beastly cheesemon-
gers, and greasy butchers and tallow-chandlers. However, niece, I can't help differing a little in opinion from
you in this matter. My experunce and sagucity makes
me still suspect, that there is something more between
her and that Lovewell, notwithstanding this affair of Sir
John. I had my eye upon them the whole time of breakfast. Sir John, I observed, looked a little confounded, indeed, though I knew nothing of what had passed in the
garden. You seemed to sit upon thorns too : but Fanny
and Mr. Lovewell made quite another guess sort of a
figur ; and were as perfect a pictur of two distrest lovers,
as if it had been drawn by Raphael Angelo. As to Sir
John and Fanny, I want a matter of fact.

Miss Ster. Matter of fact, madam? Did not I come
unexpectedly upon them? Was not Sir John kneeling
at her feet, and kissing her hand? Did not he look all
love, and she all confusion? Is not that a matter of fact?
and did not Sir John, the moment that papa was called
out of the room to the lawyermen, get up from breakfast,
and follow him immediately? And I warrant you, that

by this time he has made proposals to him to marry my sister—oh, that some other person, an earl, or a duke, would make his addresses to me, that I might be revenged on this monster!

Mrs. Hei. Be cool, child! you *shall* be Lady Melvil, in spite of all their cabillins, if it costs me ten thousand pounds to turn the scale. Sir John may apply to my brother, indeed; but I'll make them all know who governs in this fammaly.

Miss Ster. As I live, madam, yonder comes Sir John. A base man! I can't endure the sight of him. I'll leave the room this instant.   [*Disordered.*

Mrs. Hei. Poor thing! Well, retire to your own chamber, child. I'll give it him, I warrant you; and by and by I'll come and let you know all that has past between us.

Miss Ster. Pray do, madam! [*Looking back.*] A vile wretch!   [*Exit in a rage,* R.

Enter SIR JOHN MELVIL, L.

Sir John. Your most obedient humble servant, madam!
      [*Bowing very respectfully.*

Mrs. Hei. Your servant, Sir John!
      [*Dropping a half courtsey and pouting.*

Sir John. Miss Sterling's manner of quitting the room on my approach, and the visible coldness of your behaviour to me, madam, convince me that she has acquainted you with what passed this morning.

Mrs. Hei. I am very sorry, Sir John, to be made acquainted with any thing that should induce me to change the opinion, which I could always wish to entertain of a person of qualaty.   [*Pouting.*

Sir John. It has always been my ambition to merit the best opinion from Mrs. Heidelberg; and when she comes to weigh all circumstances, I flatter myself—

Mrs. Hei. You *do* flatter yourself, if you imagine that I can approve of your behaviour to my niece, Sir John. And give me leave to tell you, Sir John, that you have been drawn into an action much beneath you, Sir John; and that I look upon every injury offered to Miss Betty Sterling, as an affront to myself, Sir John.   [*Warmly.*

Sir John. I would not offend you for the world, madam! but when I am influenced by a partiality for another, how-

ever ill-founded, I hope your discernment and good sense
will think it rather a point of honour to renounce engagements, which I could not fulfil so strictly as I ought ; and
that you will excuse the change in my inclinations, since
the new object, as well as the first, has the honour of being your niece, madam.

Mrs. Hei. I disclaim her as a niece, Sir John ; Miss
Sterling disclaims her as a sister, and the whole fammaly
must disclaim her, for her monstrous baseness and treachery.

Sir John. Indeed, she has been guilty of none, madam.
Her hand and her heart are, I am sure, entirely at the
disposal of yourself and Mr. Sterling.

Enter STERLING, L. U. E.

And if you should not oppose my inclinations, I am sure
of Mr. Sterling's consent, Madam.

Mrs. Hei. Indeed!

Sir John. Quite certain, Madam.

Ster. [*Behind.*] So! they seem to be coming to terms
already. I may venture to make my appearance.

Mrs. Hei. To marry Fanny ?

[*Sterling advances by degrees.*

Sir John. Yes, madam.

Mrs. Hei. My brother has given his consent, you say ?

Sir John. In the most ample manner, with no other re-
striction than the failure of your concurrence, madam.
[*Sees Ster.*] Oh, here's Mr. Sterling, who will confirm
what I have told you.

Mrs. Hei. What! have you consented to give up your
own daughter in this manner, brother ?

Ster. Give her up ! no, not give her up, sister ; only in
case that you—[*Apart to Sir John.*] Zounds! I am afraid
you have said too much, Sir John.

Mrs. Hei. Yes, yes. I see now that it is true enough
what my niece told me. You are all plottin and caballin
against her.—Pray, does Lord Ogleby know of this affair?

Sir John. I have not yet made him acquainted with it,
madam.

Mrs. Hei. No, I warrant you, I thought so.—And so his
lordship and myself, truly are not to be consulted till the
last.

E

Ster. What! did you not consult my lord? Oh! fie for shame, Sir John!

Sir John. Nay, but Mr. Sterling—

Mrs. Hei. We, who are the persons of most coi sequence and experunce in the two fammalies, are to know nothing of the matter, 'till the whole is as good as concluded upon. But his lordship, I am sure, will have more generosaty than to countenance such a perceding. And I could not have expected such behaviour from a person of your quality, Sir John—and as for you, brother—

Ster. Nay, nay, but hear me, sister!

Mrs. Hei. I am perfectly ashamed of you—have you no spurrit? no more concern for the honour of our fammaly than to consent—

Ster. Consent? I consent? As I hope for mercy, I never gave my consent. Did I consent, Sir John?

Sir John. Not absolutely, without Mrs. Heidelberg's consent. But in case of her approbation—

Ster. Ay, I grant you, if my sister approved—But that's quite another thing, you know—   [*To Mrs. Heidelberg.*

Mrs. Hei. Your sister approve, indeed!—I thought you knew her better, brother Sterling?—What! approve of having your eldest daughter returned upon your hands, and exchanged for the younger? I am surprised how you could listen to such a scandalous proposal.

Ster. I tell you, I never did listen to it. Did not I say that I would be entirely governed by my sister, Sir John? and unless she agreed to your marrying Fanny—

Mrs. Hei. I agree to his marrying Fanny? abominable! The man is absolutely out of his senses. Can't that wise head of yours foresee the consequences of all this, brother Sterling? Will Sir John take Fanny without a fortin? No! After you have settled the largest part of your property on your youngest daughter, can there be an equal portion left for the eldest? No! Does not this overturn the whole systum of the fammaly? Yes, yes, yes! You know I was always for my niece Betsy's marrying a person of the very first qualaty. That was my maxum: and therefore, much the largest settlement was, of course, to be made upon her. As for Fanny, if she could, with a fortune of twenty or thirty thousand pounds, get a knight, or a member of parliament, or a rich common-councilman for a husband, I thought it might do very well.

Sir John. But if a better match should offer itself, why should it not be accepted, madam?

Mrs. Hei. What, at the expense of her elder sister! Oh, fie, Sir John! How could you bear to hear of such an indignaty, brother Sterling?

Ster. I! Nay, I sha'n't hear of it, I promise you. I can't hear of it, indeed, Sir John.

Mrs. Hei. But you have heard of it, brother Sterling. You know you have; and sent Sir John to propose it to me. But if you can give up your daughter, I sha'n't forsake my niece, I assure you. Ah! if my poor dear Mr. Heidelberg and our sweet babes had been alive, he would not have behaved so.

Ster. Did I, Sir John?—[*Apart to him.*] Nay, speak! —Bring me off, or we are ruined.

Sir John. Why, to be sure, to speak the truth—

Mrs. Hei. To speak the truth, I'm ashamed of you both. But have a care what you are about, brother! have a care, I say. The counsellors are in the house, I hear; and if everything is not settled to my liking, I'll have nothing more to say to you, if I live these hundred years. I'll go over to Holland, and settle with Mr. Vanderspracken, my poor husband's first cousin, and my own fammaly shall never be the better for a farden of my money, I promise you.   [*Exit*, R.

Ster. I thought so. I knew she would never agree to it.

Sir John. 'Sdeath, how unfortunate! what can we do, Mr. Sterling?

Ster. Nothing.

Sir John. What, must our agreement break off the moment it is made, then?

Ster. It can't be helped, Sir John. The family, as I told you before, have great expectations from my sister; and if this matter proceeds, you hear yourself that she threatens to leave us. My brother Heidelberg was a warm man, a very warm man; and died worth a plum, at least; a plum! ay, I warrant you, he died worth a plum and a half.

Sir John. Well; but if I—

Ster. And then, my siste· has three or four very good mortgages, a deal of money in the three per cents., and

old South Sea annuities, besides large concerns in the
Dutch and French funds. The greatest part of all this
she means to leave to our family.

Sir John. I can only say, sir—

Ster. Why, your offer of the difference of thirty thousand was very fair and handsome, to be sure, Sir John.

Sir John. Nay, but I am even willing to—

Ster. Ay, but if I was to accept it against her will, I
might lose above a hundred thousand; so you see the balance is against you, Sir John.

Sir John. But is there no way, do you think, of prevail-
ing on Mrs. Heidelberg to grant her consent?

Ster. I am afraid not. However, when her passion is
a little abated—for she's very passionate—you may try
what can be done : but you must not use my name any
more, Sir John.

Sir John. Suppose I was to prevail on Lord Ogleby to
apply to her, do you think that would have any influence
over her?

Ster. I think he would be more likely to persuade her
to it than any person in the family. She has a great respect for Lord Ogleby. She loves a lord.

Sir John. I'll apply to him this very day. And if he
should prevail on Mrs. Heidelberg, I may depend on your
friendship, Mr. Sterling?

Ster. Ay, ay, I shall be glad to oblige you, when it is
in my power; but as the account stands now, you see it is
not upon the figures. And so, your servant, Sir John.
                                                    [*Exit, L.*

Sir John. What a situation am I in! Breaking off with
her whom I was bound by treaty to marry; rejected by
the object of my affections ; and embroiled by this turbu-
lent woman, who governs the whole family. And yet op-
position, instead of smothering, increases my inclination.
I must have her. I'll apply immediately to Lord Ogleby;
and if he can but bring over the aunt to our party, her
influence will overcome the scruples and delicacy of my
dear Fanny, and I shall be the happiest of mankind.
                                                    [*Exit, L.*

END OF ACT III

A C T   I V.

Scene I.—*A Room*

Enter Sterling, Mrs. Heidelberg, *and* Miss Sterling, R.

Ster. What! will you send Fanny to town, sister?

Mrs. Hei. To-morrow morning. I've given orders about it already.

Ster. Indeed?

Mrs. Hei. Posatively.

Ster. But consider, sister, at such a time as this, what an odd appearance it will have.

Mrs. Hei. Not half so odd as her behaviour, brother. This time was intended for happiness, and I'll keep no incendiaries here to destroy it. I insist on her going off to-morrow morning.

Ster. I'm afraid this is all your doing, Betsy.

Miss Ster. (R. C.) No, indeed, papa. My aunt knows that it is not. For all Fanny's buseness to me, I am sure I would not do or say anything to hurt her with you or my aunt, for the world.

Mrs. Hei. (C.) Hold your tongue, Betsy! I will have my way. When she is packed off, everything will go on as it should do. Since they are at their intrigues, I'll let them see that we can act with vigur on our part; and sending her out of the way shall be the purliminary step to all the rest of my proceedings.

Ster. (L. C.) Well, but sister—

Mrs. Hei. It does not signify talking, brother Sterling, for I'm resolved to be rid of her, and I will. [*To Miss Ster.*] Come along, child. The postman shall be at the door by six o'clock in the morning; and if Miss Fanny does not get into it, why, I will—and so there's an end of the matter. [*Bounces out the room with Miss Sterling.* R.

Re-enter Mrs. Heidelberg, R.

(R.) One word more, brother Sterling! I expect that you will take your eldest daughter in your hand, and make a formal complaint to Lord Ogleby of Sir John Melvil's behaviour. Do this, brother; show a proper regard for the

honour of your fammaly yourself, and I shall throw in my mite to the raising of it.   If not—but now you know my mind.   So act as you please, and take the consequences.
[Exit, R.

Ster. The devil's in the women for tyranny! Mothers, wives, mistresses, or sisters, they always will govern us. As to my sister Heidelberg, she knows the strength of her purse, and domineers upon the credit of it.   " I will do this," and " You shall do that," and " You shall do t'other, or else the fammaly sha'n't have a farden of"—[*Mimicking.*]—So absolute with her money!—But, to say the truth, nothing but money can make us absolute, and so we must e'en make the best of her.
[*Exit*, L.

SCENE II.—A *Garden.*

Enter LORD OGLEBY *and* CANTON, L.

Lord Ogl. What !   Mademoiselle Fanny to be sent a-way!   Why?   wherefore?   What's the meaning of all this?
Cant. Je ne sçais pas.   I know nothing of it.
Lord Ogl. It can't be—it shan't be.   I protest against the measure.   She's a fine girl, and I had much rather that the rest of the family were annihilated, than that she should leave us.   Her vulgar father, that's the very abstract of 'Change Alley—the aunt, that's always endeavouring to be a fine lady—and the pert sister, for ever showing that she is one, are horrid company, indeed, and without her would be intolerable.   Ah, la petite Fanchon! she's the thing; isn't she Cant.?
Cant. Dere is very good sympatie entre vous and dat young lady, mi lor.
Lord Ogl. I'll not be left among these Goths and Vandals, your Sterlings, your Heidelbergs, and Devilbergs—if she goes, I'll positively go too.
Cant. In de same post-chay, my lor ?   You have no objection to dat I believe, nor mademoiselle neider too—ha! ha! ha!
Lord Ogl. Pr'ythee   hold   thy   foolish   tongue, Cant. Does thy Swiss stupidity imagine that I can see and talk with a fine girl without desires ?   My eyes are involuntarily attracted by beautiful objects.   I fly as naturally to a fine girl—

Cant. As de fine girl to you, my lor : ha, ha, ha! you always fly togedre like un pair de pigeons.

Lord Ogl. Like un pair de pigeons—[*mocks him.*]—Vous etes un sot, Mons. Canton—Thou art always dreaming of my intrigues, and never seest me *badiner*, but you suspect mischief, you old fool, you.

Cant. I am fool, I confess, but not always fool in dat, mi lor, he, he, he!

Lord Ogl. He, he, he! Thou art incorrigible, but thy absurdities amuse one. Thou art like my rappee here, [*takes out his box,*] a most ridiculous superfluity, but a pinch of thee, now and then, is a more delicious treat.

Cant. You do me great honneur, mi lor.

Lord Ogl. 'Tis fact, upon my soul. Thou art properly my cephalic snuff, and art no bad medicine against megrims, vertigoes, and profound thinking—ha, ha, ha!

Cant. Your flatterie, mi lor, vil make me too prode.

Lord Ogl. The girl has some little partiality for me, to be sure : but pr'ythee, Cant., is not that Miss Fanny yonder ?

Cant. [*Looking with a glass.*] En verité, 'tis she, mi lor —'tis one of the pigeons—de pigeons d'amour.

Lord Ogl. Don't be ridiculous, you old monkey.

[*Smiling.*

Cant. I am monkée, I am ole, but I have eye, I have ear, and little understand, now and den.

Lord Ogl. Taisez vous, béte !

Cant. Elle vous attend, mi lor.—She vil make a love to you.

Lord Ogl. Will she ? Have at her then ! A fine girl can't oblige me more.—Egad, I find myself a little enjoué —come along Cant.! she is but in the next walk—but there is such a deal of this damned crinkum-crankum, as Sterling calls it, that one sees people for half an hour before one can get to them—Allons, Mons. Canton, allons donc !   [*Exeunt, singing in French*, R.

SCENE III.—*Another part of the Garden.*

Enter Lovewell *and* Fanny, L.

Lov. My dear Fanny, I cannot bear your distress ! it overcomes all my resolutions, and I am prepared for the discovery.

Fanny. But how can it be effected before my departure?

Lov. I'll tell you.—Lord Ogleby seems to entertain a visible partiality for you; and notwithstanding the peculiarities of his behaviour, I am sure that he is humane at the bottom. He is vain to an excess; but withal, extremely good-natured, and would do any thing to recommend himself to a lady.---Do you open the whole affair of our marriage to him immediately. It will come with more irresistible persuasion from you than myself; and I doubt not but you'll gain his friendship and protection at once.—His influence and authority will put an end to Sir John's solicitations, remove your aunt's and sister's unkindness and suspicions, and, I hope, reconcile your father and the whole family to our marriage.

Fanny. Heaven grant it! Where is my lord?

Lov. I have heard him and Canton, since dinner, singing French songs under the great walnut tree by the parlour door. If you meet with him in the garden, you may disclose the whole immediately.

Fanny. Dreadful as the task is, I'll do it.—Any thing is better than this continual anxiety.

Lov. By that time the discovery is made, I will appear to second you.—Ha! there comes my lord.—Now, my dear Fanny, summon up all your spirits, plead our cause powerfully, and be sure of success.   [*Going,* R.

Fanny. Ay, don't leave me!

Lov. Nay, you must let me.

Fanny. Well, since it must be so, I'll obey you, if I have the power. Oh, Lovewell!

Lov. Consider, our situation is very critical. To-morrow morning is fixed for your departure, and if we lose this opportunity, we may wish in vain for another. He approaches—I must retire.—Speak, my dear Fanny, speak and make us happy!   [*Exit,* R.

Fanny. Good heaven, what a situation am I in! what shall I do? what shall I say to him! I am all confusion.

Enter LORD OGLEBY *and* CANTON.

Lord Ogl. To see so much beauty so solitary, madam, is a satire upon mankind, and 'tis fortunate that one man has roken in upon your reverie, for the credit of our sex. I say *one,* madam, for poor Canton, here, from age and infirmities, stands for nothing.

Cant. Noting at all, indeed.

Fanny. Your lordship does me great honour.—I had a favour to request, my lord!

Lord Ogl. A favour, madam!—To be honoured with your commands, is an inexpressible favour done to me, madam.

Fanny. If your lordship could indulge me with the honour of a moment's—What's the matter with me? [*Aside.*

Lord Ogl. The girl's confused—he!—here's something in the wind, faith—I'll have a tête-à-tête with her—allez vous en! [*To Cant.*

Cant. I go—ah, pauvre mademoiselle! my lor, have pitié upon the poor *pigeone!*

Lord Ogl. I'll knock you down, Cant., if you are impertinent. [*Smiling.*

Cant. Den I mus avay.—[*Shuffles along.*]—You are mosh please, for all dat. [*Aside and exit.*

Fanny. I shall sink with apprehension. [*Aside.*

Lord Ogl. What a sweet girl! she's a civilized being, and atones for the barbarism of the rest of the family.

Fanny. My lord, I— [*She curtseys and blushes.*

Lord Ogl. [*Addressing her.*] I look upon it, madam, to be one of the luckiest circumstances of my life, that I have this moment the honour of receiving your commands, and the satisfaction of confirming with my tongue, what my eyes perhaps have but too weakly expressed—that I am literally—the humblest of your servants.

Fanny. I think myself greatly honoured by your lordship's partiality to me; but it distresses me, that I am obliged in my present situation to apply to it for protection.

Lord Ogl. I am happy in your distress, madam, because it gives me an opportunity to shew my zeal. Beauty to me is a religion in which I was born and bred a bigot, and would die a martyr.—I'm in tolerable spirits, faith! [*Aside.*

Fanny. There is not perhaps at this moment a more distressed creature than myself. Affection, duty, hope, despair, and a thousand different sentiments, are struggling in my bosom; and even the presence of your lordship, to whom I have flown for protection, adds to my perplexity.

Lord Ogl. Does it, madam? Venus forbid!—My old

fault ; the devil's in me, I think, for perplexing young women. [*Aside and smiling.*]—Take courage, madam! dear
Miss Fanny, explain. You have a powerful advocate in
my breast, I assure you—my heart, madam—I am attached to you by all the laws of sympathy and delicacy.
By my honour, I am.

Fanny. Then I will venture to unburthen my mind.—
Sir John Melvil, my lord, by the most misplaced and mis-
timed declaration of affection for me, has made me the un-
happiest of women.

Lord Ogl. How, madam! has Sir John made his addresses to you ?

Fanny. He has, my lord, in the strongest terms. But
I hope it is needless to say, that my duty to my family,
love to my sister, and regard to the whole family, as well
as the great respect I entertain for your lordship [*curtsey-
ing*], made me shudder at his addresses.

Lord Ogl. Charming girl!—Proceed, my dear Miss
Fanny, proceed !

Fanny. In a moment—give me leave, my lord !—but if
what I have to disclose should be received with anger or
displeasure—

Lord Ogl. Impossible, by all the tender powers !—
speak, I beseech you, or I shall divine the cause before
you utter it.

Fanny. Then, my lord, Sir John's addresses are not only shocking to me in themselves, but are more particularly
disagreeable to me at this time—as—as—   [*Hesitating.*

Lord Ogl. As what, madam ?

Fanny. As—pardon my confusion—I am entirely devoted to another.

Lord Ogl. [*Aside.*] If this is not plain, the devil's in it.
—But tell me, my dear Miss Fanny, for I must know :
tell me the how, the when, and the where—Tell me—

Enter CANTON *hastily.*

Cant. My lor, my lor, my lor!

Lord Ogl. Damn your Swiss impertinence ! how durst
you interrupt me, in the most critical melting moment
that ever love and beauty honoured me with?

Cant. I demande pardonne, my lor! Sir John Melvil.

my lor, sent me to beg you do him de honneur to speak a little to your lordship.

Lord Ogl. I'm not at leisure—I'm busy—Get away, you stupid old dog, you Swiss rascal, or I'll—

Cant. Fort bien, my lor.   [*Canton goes out on tiptoe.*

Lord Ogl. By the laws of gallantry, madam, this interruption should be death ; but as no punishment ought to disturb the triumph of the softer passions, the crimi nal is pardoned and dismissed. Let us return, madam, t the highest luxury of exalted minds—a declaration of love from the lips of beauty.

Fanny. The entrance of a third person has a little re lieved me, but I cannot go through with it—and yet I must open my heart with a discovery, or it will break with its burthen.

Lord Ogl. [*Aside.*] What passion in her eyes! I am alarmed to agitation.—[*Aloud.*] I presume, madam, (and as you have flattered me by making me a party concern ed, I hope you'll excuse the presumption,) that—

Fanny. Do you excuse my making you a party concerned, my lord, and let me interest your heart in my behalf, as my future happiness or misery in a great measure depend—

Lord Ogl. Upon me, madam ?

Fanny. Upon you, my lord.   [*Sighs.*

Lord Ogl. [*Aside.*] There's no standing this : I have caught the infection—her tenderness dissolves me. [*Sighs.*

Fanny. And should you too severely judge of a rash action which passion prompted, and modesty has long concealed—

Lord Ogl. [*Taking her hand.*] Thou amiable creature—command my heart, for it is vanquished—speak but thy virtuous wishes, and enjoy them.

Fanny. I cannot, my lord—indeed, I cannot—Mr. Lovewell must tell you my distresses—and when you know them—pity and protect me.   [*Exit in tears*, R.

Lord Ogl. [*Alone.*] How the devil could I bring her to this ? It is too much—too much—I can't bear it—I must give way to this amiable weakness. [*Wipes his eyes.*] My heart overflows with sympathy, and I feel every tenderness I have inspired. How blind have I been to the deso ation I have made ! How could I possibly imagine that a little partial attention and tender civilities to tl.is young creature should have gathered to this burst of passion! Can I be a man and withstand it?—No—I'll sacrifice the whole sex to her. But here comes the father, quite *apropos.* I'll open the matter immediately, settle the business with him, and take the sweet girl down to Ogleby House to-morrow morning—but what the devil! Miss Sterling too! What mischief's in the wind now?

Enter. STERLING *and* MISS STERLING, L.

Ster. My lord, your servant! I am attending my daughter here upon rather a disagreeable affair. Speak to his lordship, Betsy.

Lord Ogl. Your eyes, Miss Sterling—for I always read the eyes of a young lady—betray some little emotion.—What are your commands, madam?

Miss Ster. I have but too much cause for my emotion, my lord!

Lord Ogl. I cannot commend my kinsman's behaviour, madam. He has behaved like a false knight, I must confess. I have heard of his apostacy. Miss Fanny has informed me of it.

Miss Ster. Miss Fanny's baseness has been the cause of Sir John's inconstancy.

Lord Ogl. Nay, now, my dear Miss Sterling, your passion transports you too far. Sir John may have entertained a passion for Miss Fanny, but believe me, my dear Miss Sterling, believe me, Miss Fanny has no passion for Sir John. She has a passion, indeed, a most tender passion. She has opened her whole soul to me, and I know where her affections are placed.   [*Conceitedly.*

Miss Ster. Not upon Mr. Lovewell, my lord; for I have great reason to think that her seeming attachment to him, is, by his consent, made use of as a blind to cover her designs upon Sir John.

Lord Ogl. Lovewell! No, poor lad! She does not think of him.   [*Smiling.*

Miss Ster. Have a care, my lord, that both the families are not made the dupes of Sir John's artifice, and my sister's dissimulation! You don't know her—indeed, my lord, you don't know her—a base, insinuating, perfidious!—It is too much—She has been beforehand with me, I perceive. Such unnatural behaviour to me!—But since I see I can have no redress, I am resolved that some way or other I will have revenge.   [*Exit, l..*

Ster. This is foolish work, my lord.

Lord Ogl. I have too much sensibility to bear the tears of beauty.

Ster. It is touching, indeed, my lord—and very moving for a father.

Lord Ogl. To be sure, sir!—You must be distressed beyond measure!—Wherefore, to divert your too exquisite feeling, suppose we change the subject, and proceed to business.

Ster. With all my heart, my lord.

Lord Ogl. You see, Mr. Sterling, we can make no union in our families by the proposed marriage.

Ster. And very sorry am I to see it, my lord.

Lord Ogl. Have you set your heart upon being allied to our house, Mr. Sterling?

Ster. 'Tis my only wish, at present, my omnium, as I may call it.

Lord Ogl. Your wishes shall be fulfilled.

Ster. Shall they, my lord!—but how—how?

Lord Ogl. I'll marry in your family.

Ster. What! my sister Heidelberg?

Lord Ogl. You throw me into a cold sweat, Mr. Sterling. No, not your sister—but your daughter.

Ster. My daughter?

Lord Ogl. Fanny!—now the murder's out!

Ster. What, *you*, my lord?—

Lord Ogl. Yes—I, I, Mr. Sterling!

Ster. No, no, my lord—that's too much.   [*Smiling.*

Lord Ogl. Too much?—I don't comprehend you.

Ster. What, you, my lord, marry my Fanny!—Bless me, what will the folks say?

Lord Ogl. Why, what will they say?

Ster. That you're a bold man, my lord—that's all.

Lord Ogl. Mr. Sterling, this may be city wit, for aught I know—Do you court my alliance?

Ster. To be sure, my lord.

Lord Ogl. Then I'll explain.—My nephew won't marry your oldest daughter—nor I neither—Your youngest daughter won't marry him—I will marry your **youngest daughter**.

Ster. What ! with a youngest daughter's fortune, my lord ?

Lord Ogl. With any fortune, or no fortune at all, sir. Love is the idol of my heart, and the demon Interest sinks before him. So, sir, as I said before, I will marry your youngest daughter; your youngest daughter will marry me—

Ster. Who told you so, my lord ?

Lord Ogl. Her own sweet self, sir.

Ster. Indeed ?

Lord Ogl. Yes, sir; our affection is mutual; your advantage double and treble—your daughter will be a countess directly—I shall be the happiest of beings—and you'll be father to an earl instead of a baronet.

Ster. But what will my sister say ?—and my daughter ?

Lord Ogl. I'll manage that matter—nay, if they won't consent, I'll run away with your daughter, in spite of you.

Ster. Well said, my lord! your spirit's good—I wish you had my constitution!—but if you'll venture, I have no objection, if my sister has none.

Lord Ogl. I'll answer for your sister, sir. Apropos! the lawyers are in the house—I'll have articles drawn, and the wh le affair concluded to-morrow morning.

Ster. Very well; and I'll dispatch Lovewell to London immediately for some fresh papers I shall want, and I shall leave you to manage matters with my sister. You must excuse me, my lord, but I can't help laughing at the match—He! he! he! what will the folks say ? [*Exit,* L.

Lord Ogl. What a fellow am I going to make a father of ? He has no more feeling than the post in his warehouse—But Fanny's virtues tune me to rapture again, and I won't think of the rest of the family.

Enter LOVEWELL, *hastily,* R.

Lov. I beg your lordship's pardon, my lord; are you alone, my lord ?

Lord Ogl. No, my lord, I am not alone; I am in company, the best of company.

Lov. My lord !

Lord Ogl. I never was in such exquisite enchanting ·ince my heart first conce— I, or my

Lov. Where are they, my lord ?   [*Looking about.*

Lord Ogl. In my mind, sir.

Lov. What company have you there, my lord ?
                                          [*Smiling.*

Lord Ogl. My own ideas, sir, which so crowd upon my imagination, and kindle in it such a delirium of extacy, that wit, wine, music, poetry, all combined, and each in perfection, are but mere mortal shadows of my felicity.

Lov. I see that your lordship is happy, and I rejoice at it.

Lord Ogl. You *shall* rejoice at it, sir ; my felicity shall not selfishly be confined, but shall spread its influence to the whole circle of my friends.   I need not say, Lovewell, that you shall have your share of it.

Lov. Shall I, my lord ?—then I understand you—you have heard—Miss Fanny has informed you—

Lord Ogl. She has—I have heard, and she shall be happy—'tis determined.

Lov. Then I have reached the summit of my wishes—And will your lordship pardon the folly ?

Lord Ogl. O yes, poor creature, how could she help it ? —'twas unavoidable—Fate and necessity.

Lov. It was indeed, my lord—Your kindness distracts me—

Lord Ogl. And so it did the poor girl, faith.

Lov. She trembled to disclose the secret, and declare her affections.

Lord Ogl. The world, I believe, will not think her affections ill placed.

Lov. [*Bowing.*] You are too good, my lord.   And do you really excuse the rashness of the action ?

Lord Ogl. From my very soul, Lovewell.

Lov. Your generosity overpowers me.—[*Bowing.*]—I was afraid of her meeting with a cold reception.

Lord Ogl. More fool you, then.

Who pleads her cause with never-failing beauty,
Here finds a full redress.   [*Strikes his breast.*
She's a fine girl, Lovewell.

Lov. Her beauty, my lord, is her least merit.   She has an understanding—

Lord Ogl. Her choice convinces me of that.

Lov. [*Bowing.*] That's your lordship's goodness   Her choice was a disinterested one.

Lord Ogl. No—no—not altogether—it began with in-terest, and ended in passion.

Lov. Indeed, my lord, if you were acquainted with her goodness of heart, and generosity of mind, as well as you are with the inferior beauties of her face and person—

Lord Ogl. I am so perfectly convinced of their exist-ence, and so totally of your mind touching every amiable particular of that sweet girl, that were it not for the cold unfeeling impediments of the law, I would marry her to-morrow morning.

Lov. My lord!

Lord Ogl. I would, by all that's honourable in man, and amiable in woman.

Lov. Marry her!—What do you mean, my lord?

Lord Ogl. Miss Fanny Sterling that is—the Countess of Ogleby that shall be.

Lov. I am astonished!

Lord Ogl. Why, could you expect less from me?

Lov. I did not expect this, my lord.

Lord Ogl. Trade and accounts have destroyed your feeling.

Lov. No, indeed, my lord. [*Sighs.*

Lord Ogl. The moment that love and pity entered my breast, I was resolved to plunge into matrimony, and shorten the girl's tortures—I never do any thing by halves; do I, Lovewell?

Lov. No, indeed, my lord--[*Sighs*]--What an accident?

Lord Ogl. What's the matter, Lovewell? thou seem'st to have lost thy faculties. Why don't you wish me joy, man?

Lov. Oh, I do, my lord. [*Sighs.*

Lord Ogl. She said that you would explain what she had not power to utter—but I wanted no interpreter for the language of love.

Lov. But has your lordship considered the consequences of your resolution?

Lord Ogl. No, sir, I am above consideration, when my desires are kindled.

Lov. But consider the consequences, my lord, to your nephew, Sir John.

Lord Ogl. Sir John has considered no consequences himself, Mr. Lovewell.

Lov. Mr. Sterling, my lord, will certainly refuse his daughter to Sir John.

Lord Ogl. Sir John has already refused Mr. Sterling's daughter.

Lov. But what will become of Miss Sterling, my lord?

Lord Ogl. What's that to you?—You may have her, if you will.—I depend upon Mr. Sterling's city philosophy, to be reconciled to Lord Ogleby's being his son-in-law, instead of Sir John Melvil, Baronet. Don't you think that your master may be brought to that, without having recourse to his calculations? Eh, Lovewell?

Lov. But, my lord, that is not the question.

Lord Ogl. Whatever is the question, I'll tell you my answer. I am in love with a fine girl, whom I resolve to marry.

Enter Sir John Melvil, l.

What news with you, Sir John?—You look all hurry and impatience—like a messenger after a battle.

Sir John. After a battle, indeed, my lord. I have this day had a severe engagement, and wanting your lordship as an auxiliary, I have at last mustered resolution to declare, what my duty to you and to myself have demanded from me some time.

Lord Ogl. To the business, then, and be as concise as possible—for I am upon the wing—eh, Lovewell?

       [*He smiles, and Lovewell bows.*

Sir John. I find 'tis in vain, my lord, to struggle against the force of inclination.

Lord Ogl. Very true, nephew; I am your witness, and will second the motion—sha'n't I, Lovewell?

       [*Smiles, and Lovewell bows.*

Sir John. Your lordship's generosity encourages me to tell you—that I cannot marry Miss Sterling.

Lord Ogl. I am not at all surprised at it—she's a bitter potion, that's the truth of it; but as you were to swallow it, and not I, it was your business, and not mine—any thing more?

Sir John. But this, my lord—that I may be permitted to make my addresses to the other sister.

Lord Ogl. O yes—by all means—have you any hopes there, nephew? Do you think he'll succeed, Lovewell?

       [*Smiles, and winks at Lovewell.*

Lov. I think not, my lord.   [*Gravely.*

Lord Ogl. I think so too ; but let the fool try.

Sir John. Will your lordship favour me with your good offices to remove the chief obstacle to the match, the repugnance of Mrs. Heidelberg ?

Lord Ogl. Mrs. Heidelberg!—Had not you better begin with the young lady first ? It will save you a great deal of trouble : won't it, Lovewell ? [*Smiles.*] But do what you please, it will be the same thing to me—won't it, Lovewell ? [*Conceitedly.*] Why dont you laugh at him ?

Lov. I do, my lord.   [*Forces a smile.*

Sir John. And your lordship will endeavor to prevail on Mrs. Heidelberg to consent to my marriage with Miss Fanny ?

Lord Ogl. I'll speak to Mrs. Heidelberg about the adorable Fanny, as soon as possible.

Sir John. Your generosity transports me.

Lord Ogl. Poor fellow, what a dupe! he little thinks who's in possession of the town.   [*Aside.*

Sir John. And your lordship is not offended at this seeming inconstancy ?

Lord. Ogl. Not in the least. Miss Fanny's charms will even excuse infidelity. I look upon women as the *feræ naturæ*—lawful game—and every man who is qualified has a natural right to pursue them ; Lovewell as well as you, and I as well as either of you. Every man shall do his best, without offence to any—what say you, kinsmen ?

Sir John. You have made me happy, my lord.

Lov. And me, I assure you, my lord.

Lord Ogl. And I am superlatively so—*allons donc !*—to horse and away, boys !—you to your affairs, and I to mine —*suivons l'amour.*   [*Sings—Exeunt severally.*

END OF ACT IV.

ACT V.

SCENE I.—*Fanny's Apartment.*

Enter LOVEWELL *and* FANNY, *followed by* BETTY.

Fanny. Why did you come so soon, Mr. Lovewell ? the

family is not yet in bed, and Betty certainly heard some-body listening near the chamber-door.

Betty. My mistress is right, sir! evil spirits are abroad; and I am sure you are both too good, not to expect mis-chief from them.

Lov. But who can be so curious, or so wicked?

Betty. I think we have wickedness and curiosity enough in this family, sir, to expect the worst.

Fanny. I do expect the worst.—Prithee, Betty, return to the outward door, and listen if you hear anybody in the gallery; and let us know directly.

Betty. I warrant you, madam—the Lord bless you both!
                                    [*Goes out at the door.*

Fanny. What did my father want with you this eve-ning?

Lov. He gave me the key of his closet, with orders to bring from London some papers relating to Lord Ogleby.

Fanny. And why did you not obey him?

Lov. Because I am certain that his lordship has opened his heart to him about you, and those papers are wanted merely on that account—but as we shall discover all to-morrow, there will be no occasion for them, and it would be idle in me to go.

Fanny. Hark! hark!—bless me, how I tremble!—I feel the terrors of guilt—indeed, Mr. Lovewell, this is too much for me.

Lov. And for me, too, my sweet Fanny. Your appre-hensions make a coward of me. But what can alarm you? your aunt and sister are in their chambers, and you have nothing to fear from the rest of the family.

Fanny. I fear every body, and every thing, and every moment—my mind is in continual agitation and dread;—indeed, Mr. Lovewell, this situation may have very unhap-py consequences.   [*Weeps.*

Lov. But it sha'n't—I would rather tell our story this moment to all the house, and run the risk of maintaining you by the hardest labour, than suffer you to remain in this dangerous perplexity. What! shall I sacrifice all my best hopes and affections, in your dear health and safety, for the mean, and in such case, the meanest consideration —of our fortune! Were we to be abandoned by all our relations, we have that in our hearts and minds, will weigh

against the most affluent circumstances. I should not have
proposed the secrecy of our marriage, but for your sake ;
and with hopes that the most generous sacrifice you have
made to love and me, might be less injurious to you, by
waiting a lucky moment of reconciliation.

Fanny. Hush! hush! for heaven's sake, my dear Lovewell, don't be so warm !—your generosity gets the better
of your prudence ; you will be heard, and we shall be
discovered. I am satisfied—indeed I am. Excuse this
weakness, this delicacy,—this what you will. My mind's
at peace—indeed it is—think no more of it, if you love
me !

Lor. That one word has charmed me, as it always does,
to the most implicit obedience : it would be the worst of
ingratitude in me to distress you for a moment.

[*Kisses her.*

Re-enter BETTY, R.

Betty. [*In a low voice.*] I am sorry to disturb you.

Fanny. Ha! what's the matter ?

Lor. Have you heard anybody ?

Betty. Yes, yes, I have ; and they have heard *you*, too,
or I'm mistaken—if they had *seen* you, too, we should have
been in a fine quandary !

Fanny. Prithee, don't prate now, Betty !

Lor. What did you hear ?

Betty. I was preparing myself, as usual, to take me a
little nap—

Lor. A nap !

Betty. Yes, sir, a nap ; for I watch much better so than
wide awake ; and when I had wrapped this handkerchief
round my head, for fear of the ear-ache from the key-hole,
I thought I heard a kind of a sort of a buzzing, which I
first took for a gnat, and shook my head two or three times,
and went so with my hand.

Fanny. Well, well—and so—

Betty. And so, madam, when I heard Mr. Lovewell a
little loud, I heard the buzzing louder too : and pulling off
my handkerchief softly, I could hear this sort of noise—

[*Makes an indistinct noise like speaking.*

Fanny. Well, and what did they say ?

Betty. Oh ! I could not understand a word of what was
said.

Lov. The outward door is locked ?

Betty. Yes; and I bolted it, too, for fear of the worst.

Fanny. Why did you ? they must have heard you, if they were near.

Betty. And I did it on purpose, madam, and coughed a little, too, that they might not hear Mr. Lovewell's voice. When I was silent, they were silent, and so I came to tell you.

Fanny. What shall we do ?

Lov. Fear nothing ! we know the worst ; it will only bring on our catastrophe a little too soon. But Betty might fancy this noise—she's in the conspiracy, and can make a man a mouse at any time.

Betty. But I can distinguish a man from a mouse, as well as my betters. I am sorry you think so ill of me, sir.

Fanny. He compliments you; don't be a fool!—[*To Lovewell.*] Now you have set her tongue a-running, she'll mutter for an hour. I'll go and hearken myself. [*Exit*, R.

Betty. [*Half aside, and muttering.*] I'll turn my back on no girl, for sincerity and service.

Lov. Thou art the first in the world for both; and I will reward you soon, Betty, for one and the other.

Betty. I'm not mercenary, neither. I can live on a little, with a good *carreter.*

Re-enter FANNY, R.

Fanny. All seems quiet—suppose, my dear, you go to your own room. I shall be much easier then : and to-morrow we will be prepared for the discovery.

Betty. [*Half aside, and muttering.*] You may discover, if you please ; but for my part, I shall still be secret.

Lov. Should I leave you now,—if they still are upon the watch, we shall lose the advantage of our delay. Besides, we should consult about to-morrow's business. Let Betty go to her own room, and lock the outward door after her; we can fasten this, and when she thinks all safe, she may return and let me out as usual.

Betty. Shall I, madam ?

Fanny. Do let me have my way to-night, and you shall command me ever after. I would not have you surprised here for the world. Pray leave me ! I shall be quite myself again, if you'll oblige me.

Lov. I live only to oblige you, my sweet Fanny! I'll be gone this moment.   [*Going.*

Fanny. Let us listen first at the door, that you may not be intercepted. Betty shall go first, and if they lay hold of her—

Betty. They'll have the wrong sow by the ear, I can tell them that.   [*Going hastily.*

Fanny. Softly, softly, Betty! don't venture out, if you hear a noise. Softly, I beg of you! See, Mr. Lovewell, the effects of indiscretion!

Lov. But love, Fanny, makes amends for all.
                    [*Exeunt all softly*, R.

SCENE II.—*A Gallery, which leads to several bedchambers.*

Enter MISS STERLING, *leading* MRS. HEIDELBERG, *in a nightcap*, R. U. E.

Miss Ster. This way, dear madam, and then I'll tell you all.

Mrs. Hei. Nay, but niece—consider a little—don't drag me out in this figur—let me put on my fly-cap! If any of my lord's fammaly, or the counsellors at law, should be stirring, I should be perdigus disconcarted.

Miss Ster. But, my dear madam, a moment is an age, in my situation. I am sure my sister has been plotting my disgrace and ruin in that chamber. Oh, she's all craft and wickedness!

Mrs. Hei. Well, but softly, Betsy! you are all in emotion; your mind is too much flustrated; you can neither eat, nor drink, nor take your natural rest. Compose yourself, child; for if we are not as warysome as they are wicked, we shall disgrace ourselves and the whole fammaly.

Miss Ster. We are disgraced already, madam. Sir John Melvil has forsaken me : my lord cares for nobody but himself; or if anybody, it is my sister; my father, for the sake of a better bargain, would marry me to a 'Change-broker; so that if you, madam, don't continue my friend—if you forsake me—if I am to lose my best hopes and consolation—in your tenderness—and affections—I had better— at once—give up the matter—and let my sister enjoy the fruits of her treachery, trample with scorn upon the rights of her elder sister, the will of the best of aunts, and the weakness of a too interested father.

[*She pretends to be bursting into tears all this speech.*

Mrs. Hei. Don't, Betsy—keep up your spurrit—I hate whimpering—I am your friend—depend upon me in every particular—but be composed, and tell me what new mischief you have discovered.

Miss Ster. I had no desire to sleep, and would not undress myself, knowing that my Machiaval sister would not rest till she had broke my heart. I was so uneasy that I could not stay in my room; but when I thought that all the house was quiet, I sent my maid to discover what was going forward; she immediately came back, and told me that they were in high consultation; that she had heard only, for it was in the dark, my sister's maid conduct Sir John Melvil to her mistress, and then lock the door.

Mrs. Hei. And how did you conduct yourself in this dilamma?

Miss Ster. I returned with her, and could hear a man's voice, though nothing that they said distinctly; and you may depend upon it, that Sir John is now in that room, that they have settled the matter, and will run away together before morning, if we don't prevent them.

Mrs. Hei. Why, the brazen slut! she has got her sister's husband (that is to be) locked up in her chamber! at night too!—I tremble at the thoughts!

Miss Ster. Hush, madam! I hear something.

Mrs. Hei. You frighten me—let me put on my fly-cap—I would not be seen in this figur for the world.

Miss Ster. 'Tis dark, madam; you can't be seen.

Mrs. Hei. I purtest there's a candle coming, and a man, too!

Miss Ster. Nothing but servants; let us retire a moment!   [*They retire,* R. U. E.

Enter BRUSH *half-drunk, laying hold of the* CHAMBERMAID *who has a candle in her hand,* L. U. E.

Chamb. Be quiet, Mr. Brush; I shall drop down with terror!

Brush. But my sweet and most amiable chambermaid, if you have no love, you may hearken to a little reason; that cannot possibly do your virtue any harm.

Chamb. But you may do me harm, Mr. Brush, and a great deal of harm, too—pray let me go—I am ruined if they hear you—I tremble like an asp.

Brush. But they shan't hear us—and therefore I say it again, if you have no love, hear a little reason!

Chamb. I wonder at your impurence, Mr. Brush, to use me in this manner; this is not the way to keep me company, I assure you.—You are a town rake, I see, and now you are a little in liquor, you fear nothing.

Brush. Nothing, by heavens, but your frowns, most amiable chambermaid; I am a little electrified, that's the truth on't; I am not used to drink port, and your master's is so heady, that a pint of it oversets a claret-drinker.

Chamb. Don't be rude! bless me!—I shall be ruined —what will become of me?

Brush. I'll take care of you, by all that's honourable.

Chamb. You are a base man to use me so—I'll cry out, if you don't let me go—That is Miss Sterling's chamber, that Miss Fanny's, and that Madam Heidelberg's.

[Pointing.

Brush. And that my Lord Ogleby's, and that my lady what-d'ye-call.'em: I don't mind such folks when I am sober, much less when I am whimsical—rather above that, too.

Chamb. More shame for you, Mr. Brush!—you terrify me—you have no modesty.

Brush. Oh, but I have, my sweet spider-brusher!—for instance; I reverence Miss Fanny—with all my horrors of matrimony, I could marry her myself—but for her sister—

Miss Ster. There, there, madam, all in a story!

Chamb. Bless me, Mr. Brush!—I heard something.

Brush. Rats, I suppose, that are gnawing the old timbers of this execrable old dungeon.—If it was mine, I would pull it down, and fill your fine canal up with the rubbish; and then I should get rid of two damned things at once.

Chamb. Law! law! how you blaspheme! we shall have the house upon our heads for it.

Brush. No, no, it will last our time--but as I was saying, the eldest sister—Miss Jezebel—

Chamb. Is a fine young lady, for all your evil tongue.

Brush. No—we have smoked her already; and unless she marries our old Swiss, she can have none of us—
no, no, she won't do—we are a little too nice.

Chamb. You're a monstrous rake, Mr. Brush, and don't
care what you say.

Brush. Why, for that matter, my dear—where's old
mother Heidelberg's room?

Mrs. H. [*Coming forward.*] There's no bearing this—
you profligate monster!

Chamb. Ha! I am undone!

Brush. Zounds! here she is, by all that's monstrous.

　　　　　　　　　　　　　　　　[*Runs off,* L.

Miss Ster. A fine discourse you have had with that fellow!

Mrs. Hei. And a fine time of night it is to be here with
that drunken monster!

Miss Ster. What have you to say for yourself?

Chamb. I can say nothing—I am so frightened, and ↲↲
ashamed—but indeed I am vartuous—I am vartuous, indeed.

Mrs. Hei. Well, well—don't tremble so; but, tell us
what you krow of this horrible plot here.

Miss Ster. We'll forgive you, if you'll discover all.

Chamb. Why, madam—don't let me betray my fellow-
servants—I sha'nt sleep in my bed, if I do.

Mrs. Hei. Then you shall sleep somewhere else to-morrow night.

Chamb. Oh, dear! what shall I do?

Mrs. Hei. Tell us this moment, or I'll turn you out of
doors directly.

Chamb. Why, our butler has been treating us below
in his pantry—Mr. Brush forced us to make a kind of
a holiday night of it.

Miss Ster. Holiday! for what?

Chamb. Nay, I only made one.

Miss Ster. Well, well, but upon what account?

Chamb. Because, as how, madam, there was a change
in the family, they said—that his honour, Sir John—was
to marry Miss Fanny instead of your ladyship.

Miss Ster. And so you make a holiday for that.—Very
fine!

Chamb. I did not make it, ma'am.

Mrs. Hei. But do you know nothing of Sir John's being to run away with Miss Fanny to-night?

Chamb. No, indeed, ma'am!

Miss Ster. Nor of his being now locked up in my sister's chamber?

Chamb. No, as I hope for marcy, ma'am!

Mrs. Hei. Well, I'll put an end to all this directly—do
you run to my brother Sterling—

Chamb. Now, ma'am? 'Tis so very late, ma'am—

Mrs. Hei. I don't care how late it is. Tell him there
are thieves in the house—that the house is o'fire—tell
him to come here immediately—go, I say!

Chamb. I will, I will, though I'm frightened out of my
wits.   [*Exit, L.*

Mrs. Hei. Do you watch here, my dear; and I'll put
myself in order to face them. We'll plot 'em, and coun-
terplot 'em too.   [*Exit into her chamber.*

Miss Ster. I have as much pleasure in this revenge, as
in being made a countess! Ha! they are unlocking the
door. Now for it.   [*Retires.*

FANNY'S *door is unlocked—and* BETTY *comes out with a
candle.* MISS STERLING *approaches her.*

Betty. [*Calling within.*] Sir, sir! now's your time—all's
clear. [*Seeing Miss Ster.*] Stay, stay—not yet—we are
watched.

Miss Ster. And so you are, madam Betty!

[*Miss Sterling lays hold of her, while Betty locks
the door, and puts the key into her pocket.*

Betty. [*Turning round.*] What's the matter, ma'am?

Miss Ster. Nay, that you shall tell my father and aunt,
madam.

Betty. I am no tell-tale, ma'am, and no thief; they'll
get nothing from me.

Miss Ster. You have a great deal of courage, Betty
and considering the secrets you have to keep, you hav
occasion for it.

Betty. My mistress shall never repent her good op'
of me, ma'am.

Enter STERLING.

Ster. What is all this? What's the matter? Why am I
disturbed in this manner?

Miss Ster. This creature, and my distresses, sir, will explain the matter.

Re-enter Mrs. Heidelberg, *with another head-dress.*

Mrs. Hei. Now I'm prepared for the rancounter—well, brother, have you heard of this scene of wickedness?

Ster. Not I—but what is it? Speak? I was got into my little closet—all the lawyers were in bed, and I had almost lost my senses in the confusion of Lord Ogleby's mortgages, when I was alarmed with a foolish girl, who could hardly speak; and whether it's fire, or thieves, or murder, I am quite in the dark.

Miss Ster. Who's in that chamber? [*Detaining Betty, who seemed to be stealing away.*

Betty. My mistress.

Miss Ster. And who is with your mistress?

Betty. Why, who should there be?

Miss Ster. Open the door, then, and let us see!

Betty. The door is open, madam. [*Miss Sterling goes to the door.*] I'll sooner die than peach.   [*Exit hastily,* L.

Miss Ster. The door's locked; and she has got the key in her pocket.

Mrs. Hei. There's impudence, brother! piping hot from your daughter Fanny's school!

Ster. But zounds! what is all this about? you tell me of a sum total, and you don't produce the particulars.

Mrs. Hei. Sir John Melvil is locked up in your daughter's bedchamber.—There is the particular!

Ster. The devil he is! that's bad!

Miss Ster. And he has been there some time, too.

Ster. Ditto!

Mrs. Hei. Ditto! worse and worse, I say. I'll raise the house, and expose him to my lord, and the whole fammaly.

Ster. By no means! we shall expose ourselves, sister! the best way is to insure privately—let me alone! I'll make him marry her to-morrow morning.

Miss Ster. Make him marry her! this is beyond all patience! You have thrown away all your affection; and I shall do as much by my obedience: unnatural fathers make unnatural children. My revenge is in my own power and I'll indulge it. Had they made their escape, I

should have been exposed to the derision of the world;
but the deriders shall be derided; and so—help! help,
there! thieves! thieves!

Mrs. Hei. Tit-for-tat, Betsy! you are right, my girl.

Ster. Zounds! you'll spoil all—you'll raise the whole
family—the devil's in the girl.

Mrs. Hei. No, no; the devil's in you, brother. I am
ashamed of your principles. What! would you connive
at your daughter's being locked up with her sister's husband? Help! thieves! thieves! I say.   [*Cries out.*

Ster. Sister, I beg you! daughter, I command you! If
you have no regard for me, consider yourselves! We
shall lose this opportunity of ennobling our blood and
getting above twenty per cent. for our money.

Miss Ster. What! by my disgrace and my sister's triumph! I have a spirit above such mean considerations;
and to shew you that it is not a low-bred, vulgar, 'Change-
Alley spirit—help! help! thieves! thieves! I say.

Ster. Ay, ay, you may save your lungs—the house is in
an uproar; women, at best, have no discretion; but in a
passion they'll fire a house, or burn themselves in it, rather than not be revenged.

Enter CANTON, *in a night-gown and slippers.*

Cant. Eh, diable! vat is de raison of dis great noise,
dis tantamarre?

Ster. Ask those ladies, sir; 'tis of their making.

Lord Ogl. [*Calls within.*] Brush! Brush! Canton!
where are you? What's the matter? [*Rings a bell.*]
Where are you?

Ster. 'Tis my lord calls, Mr. Canton.

Cant. I com, mi lor!

            [*Exit, Canton—Lord Ogleby still rings.*

Serg. Flower. [*Calls within.*] A light! a light, here!
where are the servants? Bring a light for me and my
brothers.

Ster. Lights here! lights for the gentlemen!

                [*Exit Sterling.*

Mrs. Hei. My brother feels, I see—your sister's turn
will come next.

Miss Ster. Ay, ay, let it go round madam, it is the only
comfort I have left.

Re-enter Sterling, *with lights, before* Sergeant Flower
(*with one boot and a slipper*) *and* Traverse.

Ster. This way, sir! this way, gentlemen!

Flower. Well; but Mr. Sterling, no danger, I hope.
Have they made a burglarious entry? Are you prepared
to repulse them? I am very much alarmed about thieves
at circuit-time. They would be particularly severe with
us gentlemen of the bar.

Traverse. No danger, Mr. Sterling—no trespass, I
hope?

Ster. None, gentlemen, but of those ladies' making.

Mrs. Hei. You'll be ashamed to know, gentlemen, that
all your labours and studies about this young lady are
thrown away—Sir John Melvil is at this moment locked
up with this lady's younger sister.

Flower. The thing is a little extraordinary, to be sure
—but, why were we to be frightened out of our beds for
this? Could not we have tried this cause to-morrow
morning?

Miss Ster. But, sir, by to-morrow morning, perhaps,
even your assistance would not have been of any service
—the birds now in that cage would have flown away.

Enter Lord Ogleby, *in his robe-de-chambre, nightcap, &c.,*
leaning on Canton.

Lord Ogl. I had rather lose a limb than my night's
rest—what's the matter with you all!

Ster. Ay, ay, 'tis all over! here's my lord too.

Lord Ogl. What's all this shrieking and screaming?
where's my angelic Fanny? she's safe, I hope?

Mrs. Hei. Your angelic Fanny, my lord, is locked up
with your angelic nephew in that chamber.

Lord Ogl. My nephew! then will I be excommunica-
ted.

Mrs. Hei. Your nephew, my lord, has been plotting to
run away with the younger sister; and the younger sister
has been plotting to run away with your nephew; and if
we had not watched them, and called up the fammaly,
they had been upon the scamper to Scotland by this
time.

Lord Ogl. Look'ee, ladies! I know that Sir John has

conceived a violent passion for Miss Fanny; and I know
too that Miss Fanny has conceived a violent passion for
another person; and I am so well convinced of the recti-
tude of her affections, that I will support them with my
fortune, my honour, and my life. Eh, shan't I, Mr. Sterling? [*Smiling.*] What say you?

Ster. [*Sulkily.*] To be sure, my lord.—[*Aside.*] These
bawling women have been the ruin of everything.

Lord Ogl. But come, I'll end this business in a trice.
If you, ladies, will compose yourselves, and Mr. Sterling
will ensure Miss Fanny from violence, I will engage to
draw her from her pillow with a whisper through the
keyhole.

Mrs. Hei. The horrid creatures! I say, my lord, break
the door open.

Lord Ogl. Let me beg of your delicacy not to be too
precipitate! Now to our experiment!

[*Advancing towards the door.*

Miss Ster. Now, what will they do? My heart will
beat through my bosom.

Enter BETTY *with the key.*

Betty. There's no occasion for breaking open doors, my
lord; we have done nothing that we ought to be ashamed
of, and my mistress shall face her enemies.

[*Going to unlock the door.*

Mrs. Hei. There's impudence.

Lord Ogl. The mystery thickens. Lady of the bed-
chamber! [*To Betty,*] open the door, and intreat Sir John
Melvil (for the ladies will have it that he is there,) to appear and answer to high crimes and misdemeanors. Call
Sir John Melvil into court.

Enter SIR JOHN MELVIL, *on the other side.*

Sir John. I am here, my lord.

Mrs. Hei. Heyday!

Miss Ster. Astonishment!

Sir John. What is all this alarm and confusion! there
is nothing but hurry in the house: what is the reason of
it?

Lord Ogl. Because you have been in that chamber;

have been ! nay, you *are* there at this moment, as these ladies have protested, so don't deny it.

Traverse. This is the clearest *alibi* I ever knew, Mr. Sergeant.

Flower. Luce clarius.

Lord Ogl. Upon my word, ladies, if you have often these frolics, it would be really entertaining to pass a whole summer with you. But come—[.*To Betty,*] open the door, and intreat your amiable mistress to come forth, and dispel all our doubts with her smiles.

Betty. [*Opening the door.*] Madam, you are wanted in this room.   [*Pertly.*

Enter FANNY, *in great confusion.*

Miss Ster. You see she's ready dressed—and what confusion she's in.

Mrs. Heidel. Ready to pack off, bag and baggage! Her guilt confounds her !

Flower. Silence in the court, ladies !

Fanny. I *am* confounded, indeed, madam !

Lord Ogl. Don't droop, my beauteous lily! but with your own peculiar modesty declare your state of mind. Pour conviction into their ears, and raptures into mine.
                                                          [*Smiling.*

Fanny. I am at this moment the most unhappy—most distressed--the tumult is too much for my heart--and I want the power to reveal a secret, which to conceal has been the misfortune and misery of my—my—   [*Faints away.*

Lord Ogl. She faints; help! help! for the fairest and best of women !

Betty. [*Running to her.*] Oh, my dearest mistress ! help, help, there !

Sir John. Ha! let me fly to her assistance.

⎱ *Speaking all at once.*

LOVEWELL *rushes out of the Chamber.*

Lov. My Fanny in danger--I can restrain myself no longer.—Prudence were now a crime ; all other cares were lost in this !—Speak, speak to me, my dearest Fanny! Let me but hear thy voice, open your eyes, and bless me with the smallest sign of life !

[*During this speech they are all in amazement.*

Miss Ster. Lovewell!—I am easy!

Mrs. Heidel. I am thunderstruck!

Lord Ogl. I am petrified!

Sir John. And I undone!

Fanny. [*Recovering.*] O Lovewell!—even supported by thee, I dare not look my father nor his lordship in the face.

Ster. What now! did not I send you to London, sir?

Lord Ogl. Eh!—What!—How's this?—By what right and title have you been half the night in that lady's bed-chamber?

Lov. By that right which makes me the happiest of men; and by a title which I would not forego, for any the best of kings could give.

Betty. I could cry my eyes out to hear his magnanimity.

Lord Ogl. I am annihilated!

Ster. I have been choaked with rage and wonder; but now I can speak.—Zounds! what have you to say to me?—Lovewell, you are a villain.—You have broke your word with me.

Fanny. Indeed, sir, he has not—you forbad him to think of me, when it was out of his power to obey you; we have been married these four months.

Ster. And he sha'n't stay in my house four hours. What baseness and treachery! As for you, you shall repent this step as long as you live, madam.

Fanny. Indeed, sir, it is impossible to conceive the tortures I have already endured in consequence of my disobedience. My heart has continually upbraided me for it; and though I was too weak to struggle with affection, I feel that I must be miserable for ever without your forgiveness.

Ster. Lovewell, you shall leave my house directly,—and you shall follow him, madam.   [*To Fanny.*

Lord Ogl. And if they do, I will receive them into mine. Lookyee, Mr. Sterling, there have been some mistakes, which we had all better forget for our own sakes; and the best way to forget them is to forgive the cause of them; which I do from my soul.—Poor girl! I swore to support her affection with my life and fortune; 'tis a debt of honour, and must be paid—you swore as much, too, Mr Sterling; but your laws in the city will excuse *you*, I sup

pose; for you never strike a balance without errors ex-
cepted.

Ster. I am a father, my lord; but for the sake of all
other fathers, I think I ought not to forgive her, for fear of
encouraging other silly girls like herself to throw themselves away without the consent of their parents.

Lov. I hope there will be no danger of that, sir. Young
ladies, with minds like my Fanny's, would startle at the
very shadow of vice; and when they know to what uneasiness only an indiscretion has exposed her, her example,
instead of encouraging, will rather serve to deter them.

Mrs. Heidel. Indiscretion, quotha! a mighty pretty delicate word to express obedience!

Lord Ogl. For my part, I indulge my own passions too
much to tyrannize over those of other people. Poor souls,
I pity them. And you must forgive them too. Come,
come, melt a little of your flint, Mr. Sterling!

Ster. Why, why, as to that, my lord—to be sure, he is
a relation of yours, my lord—what say *you*, sister Heidelberg?

Mrs. Heidel. The girl's ruined, and I forgive her.

Ster. Well—so do I, then—Nay, no thanks—[*To Lovewell and Fanny, who seem preparing to speak*]—there's an
end of the matter.

Lord Ogl. But, Lovewell, what makes you dumb all
this while?

Lov. Your kindness, my lord.—I can scarce believe my
own senses—they are all in a tumult of fear, joy, love, ex-
pectation, and gratitude; I ever was, and am now more
bound in duty to your lordship. For you, Mr. Sterling, if
every moment of my life, spent gratefully in your service,
will in some measure compensate the want of fortune,
you perhaps will not repent your goodness to me. And
you, ladies, I flatter myself, will not for the future suspect
me of artifice and intrigue—I shall be happy to oblige and
serve you.—As for you, Sir John—

Sir John. No apologies to me, Lovewell, I do not deserve any. All I have to offer in excuse for what has hap-
pened, is my total ignorance of your situation. Had you
dealt a little more openly with me, you would have saved
me, and yourself, and that lady, (who I hope will pardon
my behaviour,) a great deal of uneasiness. Give me leave,

however, to assure you, that light and capricious as I may
have appeared, now my infatuation is over, I have sensibility enough to be ashamed of the part I have acted, and
honour enough to rejoice at your happiness.

Lov. And now, my dearest Fanny, though we are seem-
ingly the happiest of beings, yet all our joys will be dampen,
if his lordship's generosity, and Mr. Sterling's forgiveness,
should not be succeeded by the indulgence, approbation.
and consent of these our best benefactors.

[*To the Audience.*

DISPOSITION OF THE CHARACTERS AT THE FALL OF
THE CURTAIN.

STER.   LORD O.   FANNY.   LOVE.   MRS. H.   MISS STER.   SIR J
R.}   [L

THE END.

www.ingramcontent.com/pod-product-compliance
Lightning Source LLC
Chambersburg PA
CBHW032358020726
47499CB00008B/2801